Erotic Sex Stories Collection For Adults- We Both Cum: Gangbangs, MILFs, BDSM, Hard Anal, Femdom, Tantra, Sex Games, Orgasmic Oral & 69, First Time Lesbian (Forbidden Fantasies Series)

Table of Contents

Hannah sat alone in her two-bedroom apartment, wondering what she would do, and how everything had gotten so out of control. Boxes full of all her packed belongings surrounded her, despite having been in the apartment for almost a month now. She figured she had better leave her things packed up because unless things changed for her soon, she would have no other option but to move back home with her parents and her younger brother. She had just finished her last semester of college with a bachelor's degree in mass media. She was so proud to have gotten one step closer to her dream. She aspired to one day be an investigative journalist, and to use her job to have a positive impact on the world, but that dream had quickly begun looking increasingly bleak lately. Upon graduation, she used the last of her disbursement checks to get this little apartment, but now, after only a month, she is faced with the possibility of being evicted because she had no money to cover the second months' rent. Her eyes welled up with tears at the thought of having to return home in defeat. Her family had warned her about journalism being such a competitive work line, but Hannah had been determined to follow her dream. She was regretting that decision now. Hannah did not know what she was going to do with her life, but she knew that she needed something to survive. She did not have a job, and if she does not figure something out quickly, she will not even have a place to call home.

She furiously typed away on her phone, looking for any work she might be able to do. She reluctantly put applications in at retailers and restaurants that probably would not pay much more than minimum wage. There is no way these jobs could possibly pay the bills here, but at least it is something. Days of filling out job application after job application had seemingly led her nowhere, so she started looking into other possible avenues. She looked at everything from paid survey sites to participating in paid clinical trials. She tried to sign up to deliver food and to drive people around, but the speeding tickets she got last year cause every single one of the companies she applied for to deny her application. If only David had not tossed her away right before graduation. He had been her sugar daddy for two years and the second she got near graduation he discarded her like a used tissue, probably to get himself a newer model. She bitterly thought about David and hoped that his day was sucking as badly as hers was, but she doubted that was the case. She knew the internet held the key to thousands of lucrative options for her to come out of this on top, but she had no idea where to begin looking. After searching for hours and hours, she mistakenly stumbled her way onto a website that looked rather promising but required her to not only compromise her morals but also it would put her at risk of being heavily judged if anyone ever found out. There were pages of women to scroll through, both young and old, thin and thick, all types and seemingly from all walks of life. They were all advertising their services as escorts, and most were charging hundreds per hour. She was surprised by how classy and beautiful some of them appeared to be. A year ago, she would have never considered this an option, but now her livelihood was at stake.

As Hannah's plans for the future had begun to turn into a long shot, she steadily became increasingly desperate, and now with the rent's due date closing in on her, she was desperate enough to do almost anything to avoid having to return home with her tail tucked between her legs. She could not stand where she currently stood in life, it was incredibly embarrassing for her, and as a result she avoided her friend's. She missed going to college and living on a college campus. She missed the parties, and the activities, and clubs. Hell, she even missed going to classes. Probably most of all she missed her friends. She felt a pang of jealousy when she realized they were all probably starting their careers, while she was scared and alone wondering what to do. Fallon, she figured was probably taking advantage of her very practical, as her parents would say, paralegal degree. She was probably quickly offered a good-paying job, but the last thing Hannah wanted was a job as immoral as a lawyer's job was. Katie was probably getting prepared for medical school. Hannah did not envy her at all truthfully. Medical school sounded terrible to Hannah. Ella was probably enjoying a great internship at some prestigious company, no doubt that her sugar daddy helped her get.

She did not like how envious she felt in this moment. She was not normally like this as a matter of fact she normally would have celebrated the success of her friends. She tried to push the negative thoughts from her mind. She focused on fixing the circumstances she has found herself in. She kept trying to tell her brain that would be a much better use of her memory. She hoped none of them would ever see her like this. She felt embarrassed by her desperate situation. As she walked down the hallway, she thought about her parents, and how they had tried to steer her into the medical field. It was then that she lost all the control that she had held onto for so long now and finally she burst into tears. She did not care about what others might think anymore, and it did not matter how bad it was or how many people hated her for it. Her emotions were too volatile and sad to cope with any other emotion, so she let the determination to fix this situation overcome her. She knew what she had to do, and she was not proud of her decision, but she was confident in it.

She curled up on the edge of her bed feeling exhausted by all the stress she had been enduring. She slept for longer than she had in what seems like ages. The next morning, she woke up feeling groggy, but still with a much clearer head than she had before the sleep. She grabbed her laptop from its bag and opened it on her lap. She opened her browser and navigated back to the No Games website she had found the night before, and then she clicked the sign-up button at the bottom of the page. She paused on the first box where it asked for her name. After a moment of staring off deep in thought, she decided that Lexi would be her name in this new world she was entering. For her own safety, she was careful not to give any of her real information throughout the sign-up process. It felt as though she were creating an entire new person, but that person was also her. Once she had signed up, she considered what her next step would be. Her ad was missing one vitally important thing. So before actually posting an ad, she got up, and began digging furiously through the boxes that sat in her living room. While looking through her third box she found what she had been searching for. She emerged from the box with her arms full of all kinds of lingerie and ran with it to her room, which was the only room in the house that looked decent enough for to be the background of a photo and had a mirror.

Hannah quickly threw on her favorite set of lingerie first thing, and then found herself some black thigh-high stockings to go with it. It was a leopard print bra and panty set with a matching garter. Her C-cup breasts fit snugly in the B-cup bra, making her boobs appear to be bigger. Her perfectly round nipples were just barely poking out of the top of her bra. The garter belt and lace stockings showed off her beautiful long tan legs, and her long blonde hair fell loosely over her shoulders creating a beautiful contrast against the dark orange, brown of the bra. She ran her fingers through her hair before running to the bathroom and using some dry shampoo to add some volume. She almost began applying make-up but quickly decided that it would be a waste of time because she was planning to blur her face out to protect her identity anyways. Hannah began posing for photos while she took them herself with her iPhone. She used her bed and a chair from the dining room as props. After taking pictures of every pose, she could think of and at every angle she could think of, she plopped down on her bed and began flipping through the pictures she had just taken. Majority of them, she did not like, and those got deleted but even she could see that the few she kept were stunning. She used an app to blur her face out of the photos and immediately added them to her ad. She sat up on her bed for hours looking at the computer screen and the pictures of herself on her new escort profile. She saw someone who was not Hannah, but Lexi instead, with her bare legs outstretched and her hair falling over her eyes. She could not take her eyes off her, and she could not believe she was doing it.

Her heart pounded hard in her chest and her hands shook as she clicked the button that would make her ad go public at last. Once it was done there was no going back. She stared off in a daze of mixed emotions as she tried to process her own actions and what they meant. It had not even been twenty minutes after posting her ad when her phone began to buzz off the hook. She could not even keep up with the flow of the incoming calls messages despite her best efforts to do sp. She sat there typing as fast as she could until she had found a potential client that she felt comfortable enough to have her first 'visit' with. Part of the reason she chose him was that he said that he was only interested in receiving oral, and she thought that sounded easy enough. She knew her skills in that department were exceptional, and that made her feel more confident. He also had agreed to pay the full hour's rate without trying to barter her down like most were doing. After exchanging all the necessary details along with a few pictures, she had set the visit up for later that evening at her apartment.

Hannah looked at the clutter around her and shook her head in disapproval. She decided that she could not have company with the place in this condition. Plus, now that she had some hope that she might be able to pay her rent, she felt a little better about unpacking things. She went to work unpacking and setting up the furniture and any other big items. She unpacked a few of the boxes with home décor in them and began hanging pictures and artwork that she had acquired. She laid out a few rugs the had and she even put out her wax burners with fresh wax and tea candles. The place felt so much more like home when Hannah was done. She still had a couple hours before her client was supposed to arrive, so she began to shower, shave, and get herself completely ready. When she was done blow drying her hair she looked over in the corner of the room and saw her lingerie. She picked up the whole pile and shoved them all in a drawer, quickly grabbing one out, as she shut the door. She slipped it on and looked at herself and smiled. She was feeling nervous but luckily, she was also feeling confident and sexy, and she figured those feelings would carry her through this.

Hannah's first pay to play (oral story)

The loud knock at the door came abruptly and interrupted her deep thoughts. It startled Hannah to the point of nearly jumping out of her skin. She looked at the time and was surprised to see that it was in fact closing in on the time of her scheduled visit. It was amazing how quickly the last couple of hours had passed. She quietly crept over to the door, being careful not to make any noise just in case it was someone whom she did not want to answer the door to. She slowly leaned forward and looked through the peephole and there stood the same man from the photo she had received earlier in the day. He was an older man, most likely in his late 40s or maybe 50s. He had on a light blue button-up shirt and a pair of khakis. His disheveled hair was grey and so was his mustache and his beard. He was certainly not the most attractive man ever, but she did not anticipate that he would be. She noticed that he had very kind eyes. The kind of eyes that just shouted for you to trust them without question. Hannah quickly swung the door open and let him in. She closed it behind him as fast as possible so that no neighbors would see this older gentleman coming in her apartment. Once he was inside, he looked at Hannah with a surprised and happy expression.

"Woah, you really look just like your pics", he said in awe as he looked her up and down. "I'm Daryl by the way", he noted. Hannah giggled for a moment before introducing herself.

"I'm Lexi", she said politely. She was surprised by how calm and collected she was. She had anticipated that this would be so much more stressful than it was turning out to be. "You can come on back to my room", Hannah said sweetly while giving the man a friendly smile as she waved him down the hall and toward her bedroom.

"Alright miss", he said, with the awe still clearly in his voice, as he followed her into the first of the apartment's two bedrooms. He looked around the place, curiously peeking behind each door and into every room he could see. Hannah noticed his eyes wandering around the apartment almost frantically as if he were looking for something.

"Please excuse the mess, I just moved in", she said as she tried to figure out why he kept looking everywhere as if he expected a monster to be lurking somewhere waiting for the chance to attack.

"Oh, that's alright", he said, apparently satisfied as he brought his gaze back to his prize. Hannah apologized in advance to the man in case she starts seeming nervous. She explained to him that this was her first time ever doing anything like this and told him that she would likely have the first-time jitters. He gave her a look that let her know that he knew her struggles and he felt for her. He told her that he always gets nervous too. The kind understanding feeling between them turned to something a little confusing and hard for her to comprehend when he began undoing his belt with haste.

As he unbuttoned and dropped his pants, Hannah stripped dutifully down to the lingerie she had hidden underneath her clothes. He nearly did a double take when he turned his attention back to her and saw her outfit. The see-through lace baby doll and matching thong she had on, had clearly impressed the man who stood patiently waiting for her. When she got close enough, he reached out his hands and began touching her body with an expression that indicated amazement. As she dropped down to the floor on her knees if front of the stranger his fingers slid lightly up her body, giving her chills which made goosebumps begin popping up all over her skin. She took his still flaccid cock, first into her hand for a brief moment, and then she looked up at his smiling face seductively and she teased his cock with her mouth for just a moment.

"Are you ready", she asked the stranger as she teased him by stroking her hand up and down his thick shaft.

"Yes, yes", he said breathlessly and with a slow intentional nod. She immediately began sucking on his stiffening cock. He gasped a little bit when Hannah began working his shaft, but he quickly began enjoying her work. She listened as his breathing got heavier. He reached down and started massaging her breasts gently, circling her nipples lightly with his fingertips. The sensual feeling made her nipples tingle and they hardened almost instantly as she let out a quiet moan. She quickly swirled her tongue around the smooth cock head and slowly began to suck the throbbing member harder, pulling it in and out of her mouth over and over.

"That feels so nice", he said softly as if he were in a dream. She acknowledged him with a gaze and a nod and began to gently suck on the head of his member. She momentarily licked his balls and he moaned in appreciation. After a few minutes she was back to working the man's cock with the ease of someone who was used to doing this. Then the man began to moan quietly as he looked into her eyes. She looked back at him seductively with her mouth stuffed full of his cock.

"I...it's...ohhhh, Lexi!" he cried out in great pleasure. She took him in deep and pulled out only to plunge her mouth quickly back onto his dick hard. She began to fall into a steady and constant rhythm. Her head bobbed up and down on his erect cock for quite some time. She began to wonder when he would cum as she had begun to grow impatient and bored after a while. She was brought out of her daze when she felt his fingers run through her hair and grab some of it at the top of her head. Her attention refocused and she began sucking him harder and more passionately as he kept his grip on her hair firm. The man moaned louder and began to thrust himself into her mouth harder and faster. She gagged a little bit when he pushed as deep as his cock could go, but she quickly followed up by locking her lips around the shaft with a deep suction. "I'm gonna cum baby", he warned. She continued to continue to gently bob her head up and down on his shaft. She stopped just before she felt him blow his load into her mouth. As he did, she heard him gasp in a breath of air. She pulled him out of her mouth and licked his shaft completely clean. "I'll be honest", he began. "I have been having some trouble lately. I did not think that was gonna happen. You have surprised me", he admitted in an almost as quiet a tone as her voice. Hannah gave him a sympathetic look. "Are you going to be in town a while?", he asked hopefully. Hannah laughed.

"You'll have other opportunities", she assured him as he pulled his pants back up and buckled his belt around his hips. "This is my place and I do not plan on going anywhere for a while", she said with a smile.

"You really have not done this before have you", he asked looking doubtful. Hannah shook her head no. He asked if he could tell her a few things he knows by being a client. Hannah told him that she would be grateful for any knowledge he could offer. She explained to him that she started all on her own, with no help or knowledge of how it works. He told Hannah that she should be careful giving her address out like that. He explained to her how most girls just give a general area and direct the to the right place. Hannah listened intently and nodded. She wondered why she had not considered that. Probably due to the nerves she shrugged. He also told her that in the future she should not begin to provide services until they place the money on a table or another surface in plain view. He told her that most girls will not touch the money until the services are rendered. This all made sense to Hannah as he said it. He saw her eyes look around the room to see if he had placed the money somewhere already.

He noticed and began pulling his wallet out of his pocket. He opened it an pulled out a wad. A thoughtful looked flashed across his face and he quickly opened his wallet again to pull out another bill to add to the pile. Hannah hesitated for a moment unsure of what she should do. He nodded his head in the direction of the cash letting her know that it was okay to pick it up. She began counting it and excitement welled up in her belly in response when she realized he has left three hundred which was one hundred more than they had agreed on. She smiled and thanked the man for his generous tip. He thanked her as well and assured Hannah that he would be back if she would have him. Before walking out the door he stopped and turned back to her.

"I would suggest you contact some of the other girls on the site. Maybe someone will show you the ropes, besides you could probably use a friend being that you just moved", he suggested. Her eyes widened and she smiled.

"What a fantastic idea", she exclaimed excitedly. They wished each other a great evening as he left her apartment as swiftly as he could.

Hannah sat in her room and pondered the likelihood of Daryl's suggestion working out in her favor. She knew she needed some tips so that she could make doing this as safe as possible for herself, but she was so nervous about reaching out to these girls considering all the negative stereotypes about the girls who work in this industry. She did not want to make herself seem desperate or weak to them, so that they could come to the conclusion that she would be easy to take advantage of. All of a sudden, she realized that she could at least

15

reach out to a few of the girls from the website, without ever revealing who she was, or taking any risks. She did not have to reveal her real identity, or her newly acquired escort identity, unless she felt comfortable doing so. This would allow her to test the waters before completely jumping in. She downloaded a second messaging app to keep herself anonymous when contacting these girls, she navigated to the find escorts section of the No Games website. Hours after she has sent texts out to quite a few of the girls who advertised on this site, she finally received a response. Hannah then, without giving any details as to her motives, asked the girl if she could take a quick phone call. When the girl responded with a yes, Hannah wasted no time dialing her number. She impatiently tapped her nails onto the counter as the phone rang.

"Hello? This is Kayla", said the girl from the escort website. Hannah noticed how smooth and sultry the girl's voice was.

"Um, hi", Hannah responded taking care to avoid using her name or any other identifiable details.

"Hmmm, that's not at all the voice I was expecting to hear", Kayla said in a suspicious but teasing tone, "Are you calling about my...um..services?". Hannah's heart was pounding fast and hard in her chest, but she just let it all spill out in one long frustrated sentence, without any details of course. She told the girl about her struggles, and how she needed someone to help her get started safely. When she finished there was radio silence on the other line. "Are you there?", Hannah asked tentatively.

"Yeah", said the girl, "Send me your address and I'll come by later to talk", Kayla said before ending the call. She did not give Hannah the chance to agree or to say anything at all. Hannah found that to ve incredibly rude, but at least she was not told no. She hesitated and wondered if sending this girl her address was safe or smart. In the end she decided that there was not any reason for this girl to want to harm her, so it was worth the risk. Then, before she could change her mind, she typed the address into a text message and hit the send key. Hannah began nervously pacing about her apartment, as she did anytime, she was feeling stressed or impatient. She began wondering if she had made the right decision. She decided that there was not anything she could do to change the situation at this point, so she decided to pass the time, and distract herself by unpacking more of her things. The entire time she had spent unpacking she kept checking her phone obsessively, every five minutes or so. It was driving her crazy not having any clue when this Kayla girl would show up. She decided to ignore the messages from potential clients for a while until she had an opportunity to work this out, so she muted the app she used for client's messages. She just finished breaking down the third box that she had finished unpacking and putting the contents away. She heard a faint ding and ran to check her phone.

"OTW", the message said simply. After some deliberation, Hannah responded with an okay, before she began walking around her home and hiding anything with her real name on it, and anything of value that she thought someone might want to steal. Right as she was finishing hiding all the stuff she wanted hidden her phone dinged again. It was Kayla again, only this time she was announcing her arrival. Hannah peered out her living room window which looked out to the building's main entrance. She had made it to the window just in time to see a glimpse of a woman who appeared to be in her late twenties coming in the doors of the apartment building. Moments later there was a light knock on the door, Hannah opened the door and there stood Kayla, the girl who's arrival Hannah had been anxiously awaiting all day.

"Come on in", Hannah said smiling as she held the door open for Kayla. She walked in and took a seat on the couch. Hannah first noticed how pretty Kayla was. She was a bit older than Hannah, but she was far from the stereotypical prostitute that Hannah had imagined this girl would be in her mind. Kayla was definitely a far cry from that. She was a healthy-looking, tall, brunette with an hourglass figure. She had thick thighs and an extremely healthy bust as well. Her beautiful olive skin-tone was a perfect complement to her bright green eyes. Her long straight hair almost made it down to her hips. Hannah thanked her for coming, and Kayla just quietly nodded as she looked around the place.

"So, you need some help getting started, right?", Kayla asked. Hannah nodded. "I would be happy to give you all the help you need", Kayla said. "I remember starting out, it's hard with no one on your side, and us working girls, we gotta stick together", Kayla smiled at Hannah. Hannah could not help but to be suspicious of Kayla's kindness. She wondered why this girl was being so nice to her, what could this girl possibly want from her? She hoped it was genuine, but she somehow doubted it would turn out that way.

"Is this where you plan to work?", Kayla asked. Hannah nodded in affirmation. "You know not to ever give your address, right?", she asked. Without giving Hannah a chance to answer, Kayla began speaking again, "just give a general area, or a nearby landmark that is viewable from inside your apartment, when they say they've arrived look out your window and get a good look at them. Make sure there are no suspicious vehicles surrounding them. Once you see them, you can then invite them up if they look safe". She went on to explain that she always asked for a photo so she could compare it to the person that gets out of the car. Hannah sat quietly taking it all in as Kayla continued with tons of useful information. Every now and then Hannah would take out her phone so that she could take note of the things she did not think she would be able to remember.

"How do you know if someone is a cop?", Hannah asked. Kayla then taught her how to check a person for wires inconspicuously by hugging them. She also taught her other ques that someone could potentially be a cop. Hannah had no idea how much necessary information she was missing, and she came to realize that without Kayla's help, this venture could have easily turned into a nightmare. There were so many little technicalities to remember like the one about touching the money. As

Kayla continued to reveal piece after piece of valuable information, Hannah began to let her guard down very slowly. She finally had decided to introduce herself to Kayla as Lexi. The two girls spent hours going over the various ways to make things safer for themselves, a few times their conversations had accidentally veered off into their personal lives, but by this point Hannah did not mind in the least. Kayla had a kind and nurturing spirit and Hannah felt that she could trust this girl, so she had begun to throw away her caution.

Kayla looked over Hannah's online ad and helped her make many important improvements. They also did a rn down of typical ling or slang words that were exclusive to the escort world. When she offered to take some better pictures of Hannah for the ad, Hannah started to blush a little. Other than her mom, Hannah had always been very modest and timid about being naked in front of other women. Although Hannah did think she could use some better-quality photos for her ad. After some careful deliberation she accepted Kayla's offer, and offered to return the favor as well. First Hannah knew she would need a good strong drink to help her relax. She offered Kayla one as well, which she happily accepted. So Hannah went to the kitchen and mixed each of them up a delicious tasting coconut drink with cherries in it. Plus, it was extraordinarily strong which Hannah was certain she needed at the moment. The girls were awfully close to being the same size, so they both began sorting through Hannah's lingerie, trying things on, and taking sexy photos of each other for the ads. They were having a great time hanging out together, and they clicked so naturally and instantly. After quite a few drinks Hannah offered to let Kayla stay overnight so she did not have to take the risk of getting a DUI by trying to drive home. It felt as if the two were already becoming best friends. They cuddled up in bed together and eventually fell asleep while watching one of Hannah's favorite television shows.

The next morning, when Hannah woke up the first thing, she noticed was her viciously head pounding with a hangover as a result of the previous night's festivities. She slowly sat up in bed and noticed something else peculiar. There was the delicious smell of cooking food coming from the kitchen. Hannah's stomach growled angrily, demanding to be fed. All of a sudden, the events of the night before came back to her in a flood, and she remembered how her, and Kayla had become fast friends. Hannah walked into the kitchen excited to see her new best friend. There was a huge breakfast made that Kayla was just sitting out on the table waiting to be eaten.

"I really hope you don't mind me cooking breakfast", Kayla said. "I did not use any of your food, I went to the grocery store and got stuff to make breakfast", Kayla explained. She then sat two champagne flutes and a carafe full of something orange on the table. "I got stuff for mimosas too", Kayla said excitedly. Hannah thanked Kayla and gulped down half of her glass of mimosa in a single gulp. The two girls had a great breakfast. Afterwards Kayla said that she would have to leave soon because she had plans with a client later that day. She gave another rundown of some of the safety measures they had spoken about the night before.

"How long have you been doing this?", Hannah asked.

"A long time", replied Kayla. "Honestly, I love it", Kayla admitted sheepishly. It took me a long time to admit that openly. "I have never been appreciated in any other job, relationship, or any other role in life, the way I am appreciated in this job", Kayla explained. She went on to explain how the perks of getting pampered, getting to take luxurious vacations, and in general just being doted on in every way. Hannah did not quite understand what she meant yet, but Kayla knew she would soon enough. Kayla could see the confusion cross Hannah's face, so she decided to try to explain it in a different way. Kayla had a story that she was sure would help shine some light on the situation. what she was talking about using a true story about when she had discovered that she really loved doing this job.

Kayla gets spoiled (69 Story)

Kayla grabbed her bags as she disembarked the plane. A client had flown her out to New York for a weekend visit. Kayla was exhausted from the flight. She had not expected there to be snow, and she had not packed with the expectation of snow, so she was shivering in her light jacket as she waited outside the airport for Tate to come pick her up. When he finally pulled up, she tossed her bags into the back seat and hurried into the passenger side where she huddled close to the vent to get as much heat from it as she possibly could. Tate parked in the parking garage and then they entered the neighboring apartment building. They took the elevator up to the thirty-sixth floor and made their way to an adorable studio apartment that had a beautiful view of the city. Kayla tucked her bags beneath the bed. Once she got her things put away, Tate was already laying in the bed beckoning for Kayla to come join him. She was exhausted so Tate rearranged their schedule, so they had the time to take a nap.

When she woke up Tate informed her that they only had a couple hours before they had to be at Aska, which is one of the nicest restaurants in New York City. She was delighted to discover that while she had been sleeping, Tate took the liberty of visiting a few of the designer stores a couple blocks over and he returned with a stunning cocktail dress for her to wear to Aska. When he pulled it out of the shopping bag she smiled and looped her arms around his neck and kissed him. She tried on the dress right there in front of him. She looked in the mirror at the way the dress brought out all her favorite parts of her body. He reminded her that they did not have much time to make their reservations at Aska, so she quickly did her make-up and then called to Tate to inform him that she was ready to go. They made it to the restaurant with little time to spare. They were shown to their table immediately by the nicely dressed hostess. She began looking for the menu when Tate informed her that there was no need. He made the reservations for them to have the tasting menu. She could see the chefs cooking in the nearby kitched and was amazed by their focus and deliberation throughout the entire process.

The waitress suddenly appeared with a bottle of wine. She began explaining the bottle, but it was gibberish to Kayla, who knew nothing about wine. The waitress poured them each a glass before sitting the bottle gently on the table. Moments later a plate was brought out. On it was what looked like a bundle of sticks. Even Tate was confused on how to eat the dish. Once they had figured it out, they found that it was remarkably delicious. That course was followed by eleven more artistically beautiful and stunningly tasty dishes and three more bottles of wine. Luckily, each course had a fairly small portion so that by time they were done, they were both comfortably full and sufficiently intoxicated. Tate took her to a high-end lingerie shop on the way back to the apartment. She picked a few things she liked, and he paid for the steep bill. They made one last stop on the way back to get a massage in a Chinatown shop. Kayla spent the entire time taking in all the sights of New York in amazement. Each street looked vastly different from the last, and each one was crowded with so many people from all different walks of life. They finally made it back to the apartment and Kayla went straight to the bathroom with her bag of lingerie in hand. She tried each one on and picked her favorite to wear for Tate. It was a lacy see-through romper. It was blue and had an adorable pink bow that tied around the waist. When she came out of the bathroom Tate looked at her with desire in his eyes.

"You look beautiful.", he said dreamily.

"Thank you, I'm so glad you like them." She smiled at him.

"I want to see you in all of them.", he said hopefully.

His big blue eyes shone with excitement. He ran his hands through his wavy blonde hair. She wondered why he had to resort to seeing escorts when he was such a good-looking man who also happened to be very wealthy. She decided it did not matter to her. She loved the way he doted on her, spoiled her, and tried to give her everything that caught her eye. He pulled her towards him and kissed her passionately on her beautiful plump lips. He pulled out a long white envelope from his pocket. It was half full of cash, her payment for the weekend. He brought it to her face, and she could smell the strong odor of cocaine. He smiled at her with anticipation as she pulled the small bag of white powder from the envelope.

"Just a little something extra I threw in", he said coolly. She smiled back at him and dumped a little on the table beside them and began breaking it up with a dollar bill and a paper weight that was sitting on the table. They each did a line and then laid back to let the drugs take effect. She could feel him pressing her head down to his chest, while he unzipped her romper.

"Are you alright? Do you want me to stop?", he asked softly with concern.

"No, I like it.", she said timidly as her nerves seemingly began coming to life.

"Alright, if you're sure.", he said smiling, and then he continued with his business. She could feel the fabric sliding down her back. Once he got it around her feet the held it over the bed and they watched as the fabric fell to the floor. He grabbed her by the shoulders and pulled her in close, so that she was straddling him. His hands now were rubbing her pussy. She did not have to do much to make her body respond to the stimulus. She was already very aroused and ready to go thanks to the euphoria caused by the cocaine. He slid his hand up to her chest and massaged her tits for a moment before sliding it back down to rub her bare pussy. Then fueled by the wine and cocaine, she began rubbing her tits and arching her pussy forward, pressing herself against his boner. He slid two fingers into her pussy and she moaned in response and then she felt him flip her onto her back in a single swift motion, and just like that his face was buried between her legs.

"Oh, God", she said in a heavy voice, letting her head fall back, as she felt his tongue rubbing her pussy. Her head lolled back, but it did not help the pull of the tongue. It felt as though her head was going to roll off her shoulders. His tongue was circling around her pussy lips and he could not resist the taste of her juices. He stuck his tongue as far inside her as it would go. She squirmed with ecstasy as her pussy tried to keep his tongue out. He had to have some of her, as much of her as he could get. He shoved his tongue all the way in and then brought it out and he began licking at her clit. She cried out in ecstasy. Her orgasm was quickly approaching, and she could feel the beads of sweat forming on her forehead. When he finally did bring her to her first orgasm, she grabbed his head and his hair and screamed as she shot her whole body into an out of control orgasm. She pulled his face to her pussy and forced him to continue licking and sucking. When her orgasm subsided, she took his head into her hands and looked him in the eyes.

"I am not done yet!", she said excitedly as she pulled herself up to her hands and knees. She pulled his pants off him and discarded them to the floor. Then she did the same thing with his boxers. She took his entire member into her mouth, chocking a little as she plunged all the way down forcing his cock into her throat. When he felt it enter her throat he felt as if he were about to explode with pleasure. He could not help himself. He gripped the hair on the back of her head and forced himself down into her throat a few more times. He moaned loudly as he felt the muscles constricting tightly around his cock.

He kept thrusting his hips forward, moaning in appreciation.

"I want to taste you again", he groaned as she continued to work his cock with her tongue. She slowly and carefully scooted her knees towards the head of the bed and threw her leg over so that she was straddling hi face. Her mouth did not stop bobbing up and down on his cock a single time. He pressed his mouth against her pussy as she took his balls in her hand and began licking them softly. He was in heaven. He knew his dick was going to cum soon if he did not slow her down. The way she kept sliding her mouth up and down his dick was just too good. He could not bear to bring himself to stop her. He managed to will himself to not come for the time being, as he began to circle her clit with his tongue again making her press her hips harder against his face. He thought about how amazing she tasted and he hoped he could make her come in his face again before this was over. He plunged two of his fingers deep into her tight little hole while she sucked hard on his cocked. She moaned in pleasure, so he continued pulling his fingers out and pushing them back in repeatedly.

"Oh my", she mumbled. It was barely understandable with his cock in her mouth. He reached to the back of her head and grabbed her hair, pulling her face away from his cock.

"Didn't your daddy teach you not to talk with your mouth full?", he asked before slamming her face back down so that his cock reached the back of her throat again. Her legs began to quiver, letting him know that she was close to another orgasm. So, he pushed his fingers back inside her and repeatedly slid them in and out of the dripping wet hole. First a slight tricked of cum dripped into his mouth,

"Yes", he said as he enjoyed the taste of her cum. Then, she suddenly gushed her juices as she straddled his face. He had to hold his breath to keep from inhaling it but he did not care. He was just trying to lap up as much of her come as he could. Her legs were shaking hard and quivering as she pulled her pussy away from his mouth.

"I can't take anymore", she said breathlessly. "Just let me take care of you now", she suggested. He nodded at her and smiled. He felt accomplished at making her cum so hard. She felt her soft lips lock around his cock once more. He felt her tongue rubbing against the sensitive spot right beneath the head of his cock as she gripped his balls with her hand. He loved the feeling of her mouth on his cock. He explored her entire body with his hands and watched her lips move up and down the length of his shaft.

"She is a persistent little thing", he thought with adoration as he realized that she had been going at it for some time now. He pulled lightly at her nipple with one hand as the other cupped her ass firmly. "Do you think you can handle this?", he asked as he pulled one of those high-powered wands from a bag beside the bed. She had never gotten the opportunity to use one of those, and she was curious.

"Yes baby, I want it", she cried out. He flipped the switch and the wand roared to life. She could tell that this was going to be a wild experience. He gently used his fingers to spread her pussy open and he spit on it so that it was good and lubricated. The moment the wand touched her clit she began bucking her hips forward and shaking and moaning loudly with her mouth still around his cock. It took some effort but she managed to refocus her attention on pleasing him. Seeing her experiencing that much pleasure got him closer to coming than she could have imagined. He knew he would soon come. He began using his hips to thrust his cock harder into her mouth again as he held the wand against her pussy.. The cum felt as if it were slowly making its way to the head of his cock. He knew this would be a huge load, as he had not had anything but his hand to relieve this tension in months. He felt her fingers lightly caressing his balls as he still continued to thrust his cock into her mouth. He did not want to come yet, not until he absolutely could not hold it back any longer. The look on her face made him think she was very closeto coming again as well. The feeling of his cock being at the back of her throat, it was enough to send him over the edge, and she went swiftly with him. He bucked his hips forward as they both lost all control. He began spurting all of his cum into her mouth, and a warm sweet stream began to gush from her pussy as she was hungrily swallowing every drop of his cum with greed. She sucked it all in, swallowing it in full gulps, cleaning the remnants of his load from her throat as she looked up at him.

"Oh, my that was amazing", he said leaning back against the pillows at the head of the bed. She licked her lips and nodded as she crawled towards him to lay her head on his chest.

"I was so nervous to come here", she admitted. "I am so glad I did though", she said smiling.

"I'm happy you did too", he agreed. "Hey, that worked up an appetite for me, Are you hungry?", he asked.

"Yeah, actually I am", she said. He said he knew the perfect place to take her. New York is famous for pizza, so they went to his favorite pizza spot and they got a few slices to share. She was shocked at how big they were when he brought them to the table. They were delicious though and between the two of them, they ate almost every bite. He remembered her mentioning wanting to get some souvenirs to bring back for her daughter, so next he took her to a nearby street that was lined with souvenir shops. She ended up loading her arms with things that she liked, and he paid for it all despite her telling him that she could cover it.

"If you play your cards right, some of these men will absolutely spoil you rotten", Kayla said to Hannah as she finished telling her story. Hannah had sat quietly, listening intently as Kayla explained why she loved this job so much. Hannah understood everything Kayla had said pretty well, and she knew exactly what Kayla was talking about. She remembered the rush she felt when her sugar daddy doted on her and gave her anything that she wanted without questioning it or even looking at the price tag. She remembered how powerful it made her feel, how important she felt when he would put her on that pedestal. Even just the attention he gave her was enough to give her some of the fulfillment she was now craving to have again. The way he would ignore even the most important clients to give her his undivided attention. She doubted that most wives got this kind of treatment from their husbands.

"How do you make that happen?", Hannah asked with curiosity. She was determined to get that feeling back. Hearing Kayla's story reawakened Hannah's desire to have that feeling again. The feeling had begun to swell up inside her chest, a feeling of excitement. It felt the way someone might feel if they had won the lottery.

"It doesn't always happen, some men will be very professional about their interactions with you, and you likely will not be able to get that out of those ones. With other's it can be really simple and easy actually", Kayla began to explain as Hannah leaned forward listening with interest. "Learn their names and take a genuine interest in them. It makes them feel special, and then they want to make you feel special in return". Hannah nodded at this thoughtfully. For the first time since she had graduated and left the college campus, she felt truly optimistic about her future and her financial well-being. She looked around at her apartment and instead of feeling stressed and anxious, she felt as if she could take on the whole world and win. Suddenly, she thought about how she had begun to feel about the man who was supposed to be just a sugar daddy, how she had begun to see him differently. This thought sparked an important question in her mind.

"Do you ever catch feelings for these guys?", she asked as she considered her own feelings for her former sugar daddy.

"I have a few times", Kayla answered honestly and without hesitation. With this question a few of her former clients came to mind, and she realized that this had happened to her more times than she would like to admit.

"How do you manage that", Hannah questioned. Kayla explained that she just had to keep it in the front of her mind that the feelings would eventually dwindle and subside. She had to remind herself that she was absolutely free and living a life most women could only dream of living, and that to give that up for an exclusive relationship with one man was completely insane, especially when she could still have that man in all the best ways without having to give everything up to commit herself to him. Hannah made a mental note to remind herself of that if ever she felt the desire to emotionally attach herself to a client. She knew she had a tendency to be a highly emotional individual, and that could be difficult to manage at times. So, she could foresee the possibility of this type of thing happening to her at some point. It almost seemed inevitable in this type of job. An opposing though occurred to her as she considered how the job could also make her not want any type of attachment to any person. It was just as likely that she could become overwhelmed with having to fake interest and attachment with people she may not particularly like.

"Does sex ever begin to feel like work to you? I mean do you stop enjoying it due to it being your job?", Hannah asked. Kayla thought this over for a moment and then she began telling Hannah that thinking about the money she was making always turned her on. So even if she did not necessarily enjoy the sex with that particular client, she could still get herself turned on by thinking about the cash she would be walking away with. Luckily, there had almost always been at least one client with whom she genuinely enjoyed having sex with. She did however go through a period of time when she had begun to lose interest in sex. Thankfully, it was only temporary, and it turned out to be a rather easy fix. She just had to engage in some sexual activity that was not related to her work. The first time she did this, she did not do it with intention, and in fact she engaged in some pretty high-risk sexual behavior as a result, but it taught her an important lesson about how to, and how not to handle those situations. Luckily on her first instance of this she was able to emerge from it unscathed. However, she considered herself lucky because it very well could have easily turned out much different for her.

Kayla pondered whether she should tell this story to Hannah or not. It was a somewhat embarrassing story to tell, and she had not told many people at all for fear it could come back to bite her. It was actually fairly recent in fact and she unfortunately had to worry constantly about the possibility of it coming out into the open. She was surprised at how much she already trusted Hannah already. This girl had just stumbled into Kayla's life, and Kayla was not even completely sure why she had agreed to take on the huge job of mentoring her, and without even asking for payment in any form. She brushed it off when she recognized how good it made her feel. She wanted to help this girl empower herself. Kayla threw all caution to the wind and decided to tell Hannah the story despite how embarrassed she felt about doing so.

"I need to let you in on a few things before I tell you this story", she said to Hannah. First she made Hannah promise to remain tight-lipped about this one. She explained that it had the potential to have consequences on her relationship with her daughter. Hannah felt honored that Kayla was willing to share this clearly personal story with her. She had heard Kayla mention getting souvenirs for her daughter in the last story but decided not to ask and questions about it due to the personal nature of the topic, not that she was not curious. Kayla then revealed that at the time she had been experiencing some sort of crisis that had made her act out of character. Hannah assured her that she understood what it was like to go through that sort of thing, she had many coming of age crises in her teenage years. So, Kayla took a deep breath to calm her nerves and began at the beginning of the story.

A Naughty MILF (MILF Story)

"I should mention that I became a wife and mother at the young age of eighteen. So, I have a daughter who is now in her preteens", she admitted. She explained that she had lost custody of her daughter when she got divorced, and the court ordered that she only got to see her child when her ex-husband allowed it from then on. Her former husband eventually remarried, moved across the country and now Kayla's daughter had a stepmother and a stepbrother. Kayla tried not to complain much because they were incredibly good to her Pheobe, and she realized that the situation could be much worse. They gave her daughter an excellent life and provided her with everything she would possibly need and then some. She knew her daughter was happy where she was, despite the fact that they both wished they could see one another more often. One evening her daughter called her as she usually did each night before her bedtime. When Kayla answered the phone, her daughter's voice boomed loudly through the Phone. She could tell that Phoebe was excited but could hardly understand what she was saying at first. When Phoebe finally calmed down enough so that Kayla could understand her, she became just as excited as her daughter was. She would soon get to spend some quality time with her daughter.

Kayla was excited to be going to visit her ten-year-old daughter after more than a year had passed without seeing her. She got off the plane and met Phoebe, who was accompanied to the airport by her eighteen-year-old stepbrother, who politely introduced himself as Justin. Phoebe's father, Gerald, and stepmother, Karen were going on a vacation with Karen's family for a few days and Justin had already made plans to leave town to go on a road trip with some of his friends from school, so they asked Kayla if she would like to come baby sit for them. Kayla was happy they had asked, and she quickly agreed, she was not going to miss this rare opportunity to spend quality time with her daughter for anything. When Kayla got off the plane, Phoebe stood waiting with a bouquet of flowers in one hand and a homemade card in the other. When Kayla approached, they both had tears welling up in their eyes. Phoebe held both of her arms out to her mother with the gifts she had brought her and excitement shining in her eyes. They stopped a few times on the way out of the airport to take a few selfies together, as well as to pick up the rental car Kayla had booked for the trip. Phoebe asked her brother Justin time and time again if she could ride along with Kayla. He looked at Kayla apologetically as he explained that his mother instructed him to drive Phoebe home himself.

Kayla calmed her upset daughter, assuring her that she would be following right behind her in the rental car the entire way back. Phoebe remained a little pouty after that but did not put up much more of a fuss. Upon arriving at their house, Justin, who was a skinny young man with dirty blonde hair, dutifully turned on the oven to prepare a casserole his mother had made in preparation for Kayla's arrival. It smelled delicious and when it was done Kayla made all three of them a plate and sat them at the table. The all sat down and ate together at the dining room table as Justin went over the extensive instructions his mom, Karen had left for Kayla. Kayla felt a little overwhelmed, and even Justin had indicated that he recognized how ridiculous his mother was being. Karen had practically planned the entire week for her and Phoebe. She was thrilled and grateful to be able to spend the time with her daughter, but she was really hoping to take her to do some things that she thought they would enjoy doing together. Once everyone had eaten everything on their plates, Kayla watched television as she sat on the floor and colored with Phoebe for a while before putting her to bed at the time Karen had instructed her to do so. With Phoebe asleep and Justin up in his room, began searching the kitchen for some wine or anything else to help her relax. She looked in every cabinet, the fridge, and even the pantry, but found no trace of anything to help her take the edge off her jetlag.

"Looking for this?", a voice came suddenly from behind her. She jumped and turned to see Justin standing behind her with an unopened bottle of wine in one hand. "I won't tell if you won't", he said looking at her smiling. She breathed a sigh of relief and smiled back at Justin.

"You scared me half to death", Kayla responded as she turned to retrieve two wine glasses and a corkscrew from the cabinet. Justin took the corkscrew from Kayla, carefully opened the bottle and poured them each a glass of the wine pouring it exactly as a professional would have. "Are you old enough to be drinking?", she asked even though she already knew the answer. He just at her and shrugged as if it did not matter.

"Have you ever played spades?", he asked Kayla as he retrieved a deck of cards from his back pocket. Kayla agreed to play because spades was one of her favorite games, but she had not played it in years. They sat down at the table and Justin began shuffling the deck. She could tell he played sports. He was not as scrawny as she had first thought. Just toned and fairly thin. He had striking gray eyes and an incredibly handsome smile. Time flew as they got playfully competitive over the game. About three games in the wine bottle was empty. "I'll go grab another", Justin said nonchalantly.

"But what if", Kayla began, but Justin quickly cut her off.

"Trust me, my mom would never notice even if we drank twenty bottles. Her wine cellar has hundreds of bottles in it", he explained. "Come on I'll show you", he said as he waved her in the direction of the door that led down to the basement. At the bottom of the stairs there was a big open den like area, through one of the two doors down there was a massive wine cellar that was fully stocked with an enormous collection of wine.

"Woah", explained Kayla.

"Go on, pick any one you like", Justin urged. Kayla selected a sweet white wine that caught her eye. Justin popped it open and they settled on the couch in the den. Justin put some music on the surround sound system.

Both of their heads were buzzing from the wine. They were having a thought provoking and deep conversation about Justin's romantic life. When he asked about her love life, she told him there was not much to tell. He got a thoughtful expression on his face and then leaned in towards her. Everything in her was screaming to put a stop to this. Something stopped her. Maybe it was the wine or how cute and sweet Justin was, or maybe it was her anger at Karen and her ex that she had kept submerged all these years, but when his lips met hers, she kissed him back. She knew it was wrong but once it began, she felt as if she were powerless to stop it. His tongue gently pried her lips apart and made its way inside, pressing gently against the inside of her cheeks. She clumsily pressed her tongue back against his. He was careful and tactful, never pushing too hard so that she could come to her senses and put a stop to this madness. Her insides felt as if they were a molten lava pool ready to erupt at any moment. Justin's arms went around her and rested at her waist as they kissed.

She could feel his penis press against her thigh. He moved his lips to her neck for a moment and then kissed her on the lips again. As if she were in a trance, she mindlessly let her hand glide slowly up from his thigh, stopping at the waistband of his shorts. It was uncomfortable, and she was not sure why she kept moving forward but she did. She felt the warmth of his body as she slid her hand down to his penis. It was still partially limp, just slightly chubby, most likely as a result of his nerves. He pushed the bottom of her tank top up slightly and pinched her nipples lightly. Her head was spinning with misplaced desire that likely stemmed from the forbidden nature of what she was doing. She still had a dry mouth and no breath to give. She took another gulp of the wine that was still flowing freely through her causing her inhibitions to falter. Justin massaged her shoulders as he left a trail of kisses up her neck. Each one left a tingling sensation behind. She had gone from being shocked and disgusted with herself and what was taking place to euphoric within a matter of mere seconds. He gave her a quick but lingering kiss on the lips. Kayla scrambled to her feet unsure of what to do next. She had never wanted to be naked with anyone this bad before, but the thought simultaneously turned her stomach, or maybe it was the wine doing that. Justin was sitting on the couch and was watching her with intensity. His hand went between his legs and he rubbed himself. Kayla reached over and placed her hand on his dick. It was soft before but now he was rock hard. She was stunned by the size of his erect cock.

Kayla did not know why, but she just could not resist touching him. She slid her hand down the length of his shaft, over his balls and then on to his taint. She did not think much about it because she was completely hammered by this point. It felt amazing for both of them and she giggled out loud at this outrageous situation she had found herself in. It was at that point that Justin slowly moved in front of her. His eyes were downcast as he had her turn around so that she was sitting between his legs, facing him. He then reached over and took her hand and placed it on his dick. Kayla jumped up, momentarily coming to her senses and looked over her shoulder.

"Justin, what are you doing?", she asked

"I need this," he stated. "I need to feel your touch." Kayla succumbed slowly stroked his penis until it was as hard as a rock again. Kayla was unsure what to do next. She knew she needed to get out of there, but Justin had her fully turned around. Justin put his arms around her and began kissing her neck, and then slowly down her chest. He stopped just at her chest and stared at her nipples for a few moments. He looked her in the eyes, winked, and slowly lowered his mouth to her left nipple and took it in his mouth. Kayla's nipples were extremely sensitive, which was not a good thing when she was drunk. Her body began to tingle, and she wanted to reach over and rub herself, but was unsure of what to do or how to do it. Justin continued sucking on her nipples as he continued tracing a line around her belly button with his fingers. Kayla felt one of his fingers tickling her belly button. She could feel the warming sensation travel up into her belly. As he continued his attention to her breasts, he began pushing the other finger inside her. Kayla quickly found that she loved his fingers. She felt like her vagina was on fire. He took his finger out of her pussy and her it immediately returned to feeling normal. He put his hand between her knees, spreading her legs open wider and ran his finger slowly from her clitoris up to her anus. This was unexpected, and Kayla let out a loud yelp of surprise. Justin remained unfazed and continued to touch her as if nothing out of the ordinary had happened.

She pushed him back and he leaned back onto the couch. He then moved back in closer to her. Both Kayla's excitement and fear intensified all at once. He bent down toward her and kissed her deeply and passionately. He felt her breath become heavy as she almost began to pant, and felt every muscle in her body tensing up. She realized she was about to give in to her desire completely and she could do nothing to stop it. He gently removed his belt and lowered his pants. He gripped her hips and gently pushed himself into her. Justin slowly slid inside her as he held her hips in his hands and stared down at her face. Kayla began to relax as he slowly slid in and out of her body. He grabbed her hips and began pumping faster. She let out a loud moan as he hit her g-spot with every thrust. Justin was now fully inside her, and he began thrusting even harder. Kayla felt as if her insides were burning up with an intense sensation as she neared an orgasm, and soon she was on fire. Her head was spinning as the pleasure completely overcame her. She wanted to tell him to stop, but for some unknown reason she needed this badly. He looked up at her as he continued to thrust inside her and smiled.

"You look beautiful like that," he said to her. He began thrusting harder and harder, pounding himself into her with all the force he could muster up.

"Justin," she said suddenly. Then she weakly murmured, "please don't stop", she silently cussed herself as she knew she had meant to tell him to stop. He could see the worried expression on her face.

"Don't worry", he said comfortingly as he smiled at her and began thrusting faster into her wet pussy. After a few more minutes, he let out a loud moan, and Kayla felt his body shake violently as he came inside her. She could feel his cum gushing out and filling her with his seed. The trance she had been in was broken immediately. She ran to the bathroom and tried to clean as much of his cum out of her pussy as she could. When Kayla walked out of the bathroom, she saw that Justin had made himself comfortable on the couch and had fallen asleep. He still had no clothes on so Kayla put a blanket over him and quietly crept upstairs to the guest bedroom where she should have been all along. She curled up in bed and tried to make sense of what she had just done. When she could not make sense of it, she began thinking up ways that she could ensure that no one ever found out about what had just happened. Then she cried herself to sleep, hoping that this would not come between her and her daughter

After finishing her story, Kayla was already late meeting her client, so she had to rush off quickly, leaving Hannah alone to ponder everything Kayla had covered throughout the last couple days. Hannah did not judge Kayla for any of the things she told her, in fact she looked up to her even more for having overcame the obstacles she had to face. Taking in all that new information must have worn her out because Hannah felt insanely tired all of a sudden. She laid down, curled up in her bed and fell straight into a deep sleep. Hannah woke up a couple hours later feeling as refreshed as she would have if she had gotten a full night's rest. She got straight up and jumped into a hot shower. When she got out and dried off, she grabbed her phone to see if she had missed anything during her nap. She saw a missed call from Kayla from about thirty minutes prior so she immediately pressed the call button to see what she had called about.

"Hey", Kayla said cheerfully. "What are you doing?", she asked.

"Not much", Hannah replied trying to get the sleepiness out of her voice.

"Well, I realized that I desperately need to get my nails done, and I thought I would invite you to come along with me. My treat!", she said to Hannah in a persuasive tone. Hannah needed no persuasion though. She agreed immediately and with no hesitation and thanked Kayla for inviting her along. Kayla told her she would be there in about twenty minutes and Hannah told her that she would be ready. They said their goodbyes and hung up the phone so that Kayla could focus on driving and Hannah could finish getting ready. Once she was off the phone, Hannah ran to the restroom to blow dry her hair and fix her make-up before Kayla arrived. About a half hour later Hannah got a text from Kayla letting her know that she was pulling up to the apartment building. Hannah was already ready and waiting downstairs. She hopped into the passenger seat, sat her purse down in the floorboard, and fastened her seatbelt. The salon where Kayla got her nails done was conveniently right down the road from Hannah's apartment. The bell dinged as they opened the front door of the nail salon to go inside a were immediately sat side by side on the area of the salon that was dedicated to manicures. They were offered a glass of wine which they both accepted graciously.

After discussing a few different colors and designs and getting one another's opinions. They both settled on what they wanted done to their nails. Kayla was getting a simple elegant design with fed paint and gold glitter swirls. Hannah had a tendency to be a bit quirkier and more expressive, so she got an adorable design with lip prints for Valentine's Day which was just around the corner. A little over an hour later, Hannah and Kayla were washing their hands and showing each other their nails proudly. Once they got back into the car the conversations about their job resumed since they no longer had to worry about their conversation being overheard by patrons or the salon staff.

"Where do you live and work?", Hannah asked Kayla noticing that Kayla had never mentioned anything about this before.

"I stay in hotels", Kayla stated.

"That must be expensive! How do you carry all your stuff around all the time like that?", Hannah asked with a concerned expression. Kayla explained that hotels were the norm for working girls. She realized as she thought about it that she had actually never met an escort who had a permanent residence. She then assured Hannah that it should be fine, better actually, than jumping from one hotel room to the next. She told Hannah that she just did not keep more than she needed, which made it easier to move frequently. Hannah frowned at this, thinking that Kayla would probably be much happier with the stability of having a place to call home. Hannah pointed out her favorite sushi spot as they drove past.

"Oh I love that place", she exclaimed.

"Sushi?", Kayla asked making a disgusted face. Kayla looked surprised.

"You don't like sushi?", she asked.

"I've never actually had it", Kayla said. Hannah insisted that the go get some so Kayla pulled into the sushi bar. They went inside and both ordered a drink called oriental water, which had sake and some fruity mixers. Hannah ordered for the both of them. When the waitress brought out the sushi, Kayla admired how pretty it looked but admitted that she was nervous to taste it. Hannah showed her which to try first. She was amazed by how delicious it was, and she liked every one that Hannah had ordered for them. They ended the meal with some green tea ice cream and then Hannah paid the bill. They left excitedly talking about how great the food was. The girls had become close friends and rather quickly. It all felt very natural to them both.

Kayla dropped Hannah off at her apartment so that she could go back to her room and work. Hannah decided to finish getting her place set up and ready for her to work. She unpacked the rest of her boxes and organized everything. She looked around in the spare bedroom and wondered what she would use it for. When she got done getting her place the way she wanted it she poured herself a glass of wine and sat down to go over the things Kayla had taught her, and to reflect on her friendship with Kayla. She loved how naturally they clicked. Kayla really was a truly kind person, and Hannah was not sure what she would have done without her. She decided she probably would have landed herself into some massive trouble. She began considering ways she could repay Kayla for her kindness and help.

The following morning Hannah awoke to her phone ringing. She had been hearing it ring for a while, but she was unable to bring herself to get up until now. She rolled over and grabbed her phone from her nightstand and squinted her eyes at the screen to see who was calling her. It was Kayla, so she bolted upright and answered her phone as quickly as possible.

"Hello?", she said with the grogginess still apparent in her voice.

"Hey", Kayla said on the other line, "Sorry I didn't mean to wake you up but it is sort of important".

"It's fine", Hannah replied. "I was about to get up anyways", she lied. Kayla explained to Hannah that one of her best clients had come to see her the night before. She had been telling him all about Hannah and their friendship. Then this morning she woke up to a message from him requesting to see them both. He said that he did not actually want to fuck both of them. He wanted to take them out to a nice dinner and afterwards he wanted to watch Hannah and Kayla fuck each other. Hannah was silent on the other line as she took this all in. She had never done anything with a girl before and the idea was very intimidating. Hannah could not help but to be incredibly nervous about this proposal and she was not sure if she would even be able to go through with it.

"Hannah?", Kayla's voice called, breaking through Hannah's daze.

"Yeah, I'm still here", Hannah replied.

"So, what do you think?", Kayla asked. Hannah paused for a moment trying to figure out the least embarrassing way to tell Kayla the truth. She stumbled over her words for a moment.

"Have you ever been with a girl before?", Kayla chimed in.

"No", Hannah replied. Kayla assured Hannah that everything would be fine. She said that they really just needed to put on a show for the client. She told Hannah just how lucrative this could be. She also assured Hannah that she would help her along and make sure she knew what she was doing. "Okay", Hannah said, finally agreeing tentatively.

"Awesome, I'll be over in a bit to start your training young Jedi", Kayla replied jokingly.

Hannah got out of bed and went straight to the shower. She was not sure what Kala had meant by training, so she wanted to be clean just in case. After scrubbing herself to her satisfaction and shaving her legs, underarms and pussy, she stood under the almost scalding hot water until it ran cold. When she got out of the shower, she wrapped her hair in a towel and wrapped another around her body and headed towards her room to get herself dressed. As she stepped into the hallway, Kayla busted into her living room without knocking startling Hannah.

"Oh, sorry I didn't mean to scare you", she said. "You left your door unlocked", she shrugged her shoulders and then smiled at Hannah. Hannah told her that she was going to get dressed and she would be right back out. Hannah ran to her room and threw on the cutest underwear in her drawer, the first pair of jeans she could find, and a crop top she grabbed from her closet. She spritzed herself with some perfume before going to meet Kayla in the living room. Kayla was sitting on the couch seemingly captivated by whatever she was doing on her phone. Hannah sat beside her and Kayla showed her the screen on her phone. It was playing porn from a porn website Hannah had heard of once or twice before but had never visited. Predictably, Kayla had lesbian porn playing, Hannah leaned in to watch, silently telling herself that it was solely for the purpose of research. They watched the screen as the two girls went from kissing one another to fingering each other, then one girl began eating the other's pussy, and then that girls pulled a rabbit toy seemingly from thin air and began thrusting it into the pussy of the girl who was eating her out. The girls sat side by side, watching and saying nothing, both felt awkward knowing that they would probably be doing these things with each other soon.

"So, I spoke to Jason, that's the clients name, about when he wants to do this and he leaves town tomorrow, so we have to do it this evening", Hannah's jaw nearly dropped. She had not been expecting it to move so quickly. Kayla looked at her apologetically.

"Okay", Hannah replied apprehensively.

"He's paying us five hundred dollars each", Kayla said looking at Hannah intensely. Hannah thought of how much five hundred dollars would help her right now, and it would only take a couple hours of her time. She knew she needed to do this. Plus having her new best friend with her should provide her with some much-needed comfort.

"I'm in", Hannah said more decisively this time. Kayla sent Hannah a few links for some videos to watch that demonstrated what she had in mind. Hannah agreed to watch them. Then Kayla learned in and kissed Hannah on the mouth. Hannah kissed her back, feeling shockingly passionate in the moment. Hannah was surprised to find that she enjoyed the kiss so much she felt herself start to get wet. Kayla looked at Hannah and smiled victoriously.

"We've so got this", she said confidently as Hannah was still trying to regain her composure from the dizzying kiss they had just shared. Hannah smiled back at her feeling a little awkward. Kayla began excitedly rambling about doing a two-girl special if this went well. She seemed excited about the earning potential this had so Hannah figured it must be pretty in demand. Kayla told Hannah she would see her later and they hugged before Kayla left the apartment. Hannah locked the door behind her and once alone her eyes went wide as she took in what had just happened. She had never felt attracted to a girl before, but the kiss she had just shared with Kayla had left her craving more. She found herself looking forward to that evening. She was still incredibly nervous, maybe even more so now, but at least there was now some excitement mixed in too. Hannah made her way back to the bathroom to do her makeup and her hair. Kayla had texted her to tell her she would be back around five to pick Hannah up so they could meet Jason at the restaurant. Then she sent a pic of herself in the lingerie she planned to wear. She had on a black bra and pantie set, a matching garter belt, and some stockings. She suggested that Hannah wear the similar set she had in red. Hannah texted her back to say that she would.

Hannah passed the time by watching the videos Kayla had recommended. She was glad to be watching them alone. The few moments she had spent watching porn with Kayla had been very awkward and uncomfortable. However, the kiss they had shared made it much easier, and much more exciting to imagine doing those things with Kayla. Hannah got a little wet watching the first video, and by the end of the second she was squirming. She tried to curb her libido as much as she could, but she eventually had to get her clit sucker toy from her dresser drawer. This thing was incredibly quick and straight to the point and Hannah liked that. The moment it latched onto her clit her entire body began to shake and twitch. Within moments she was gushing. Luckily, she had the foresight to put a towel beneath the lower portion of her body before getting the toy. Otherwise, there would have been a terrible mess for her to clean. Hannah glanced at the time on her phone. She had about an hour before Kayla would be arriving to pick her up. Hannah decided it was time that she get up and get herself done up for this dinner date. She grabbed a classy yet sexy cocktail dress from her closet and slipped it on. Then she went to the restroom to freshen up and touch-up her makeup. About the time she finished getting ready, she heard Kayla banging on her door. Hannah grabbed her purse and hurried out the door. Once outside Kayla looped her arm around Hannah's.

Hannah's First Girl
(First Time Lesbian Story)

"Ready?", she looked at Hannah with an adorably mischievous smile. Hannah could not help but smile back as she nodded her head. The ride to the restaurant was spent jamming to their favorite songs. They took turns blaring their favorite songs through the car's speakers. They both sang along to every song they knew as the bobbed their heads to the music. Kayla exchanged a few texts as they pulled into the area where the restaurant was so she could find out where Jason had parked. She pulled up directly beside his huge black Toyota. They got out of the car and there stood Jason. He was a medium height, older gentleman who was not bad looking by any means. He smiled brightly and hugged Kayla first, and the hugging Hannah as he introduced himself to her. He escorted them into the restaurant where they were quickly seated at a table near the bar.

"She's every bit as stunning as you said she would be", Jason said to Kayla. He glanced in Hannah's direction and winked at her flirtatiously.

"I know isn't she", Kayla said touching Hannah's face clearly putting it on extra thick for her client. Hannah looked into Kayla's eyes lustfully to let her know she understood the role they were to play. Hannah wondered how much of it was really them playing a role and how much of it was real. Hannah could feel the chemistry between her and her friend since they had kissed, she wondered if Kayla was feeling it to. They sat and chatted and flirted with one another constantly throughout their meal. They ended up just sharing a few appetizers and having a couple drinks each.

"Would you ladies care to ride with me?", Jason asked. "I can drive you back here to your car once we finish up at my place", he offered.

"Sure", Kayla responded in a bubbly tone. "That's okay with you right Lexi?", Hannah had nearly forgotten to respond to her escort name.

"Of course, it is", she said trying to imitate Kayla's level of enthusiasm.

Kayla climbed into the passenger seat beside Jason, and Hannah got into the seat behind Kayla. It was a short ride, which Hannah mostly spent listening to the light conversation that was taking place between Kayla and Jason. They pulled in and parked in front of an enormous house. Hannah looked over the place taking in the massiveness of it. She wondered if Jason had family here or if he lived alone. If it were the latter, she did not know how he could stand to live alone in such a huge place. She marveled at the beautiful design of the place. Each detail was clearly intentional. Hannah thought briefly of her old friend Ella, from college. She had graduated with a degree in design and would have loved to have seen this stunning place. The thought made her feel a pang of sadness as she realized how much she missed the dorms. Having friends around her all the time had made living alone quite the adjustment, Hannah frequently got lonely and often had trouble sleeping as a result.

"What a beautiful place you've got", Hannah said as she turned her attention back towards Jason and Kayla.

"You haven't seen the best of it yet", he exclaimed. "I think a tour is in order", he said as he began leading the ladies through the house. Hannah noticed that Jason loved showing off. She was careful to frequently give him complements because she had already gathered that was the best way to win his favor. Jason had been momentarily distracted when Kayla gave her an expression of excitement and a thumbs up. Even though she had quickly grown bored of the tour, Hannah acted as if she were wowed by every single room for the purpose of stroking Jason's clearly enormous ego. Jason passed her a drink which she took and thanked him. He then escorted them to a room with a huge bed in the center of it. Adjacent to that room there was a lounge area which appeared to have formerly been a walk-in-closet. The lounge area had small windows that one could look through to see into the bedroom without being seen themselves. Hannah thought that was rather odd, but she made no mention of it because she did not want to be rude.

"This is where we do our thing", Kayla said to Hannah flirtatiously and with an exaggerated excitement. Hannah followed along smiling back at Kayla mischievously.

"I've been waiting patiently for this all day, and I don't know if I can stand waiting much longer", she said seductively back to Kayla. Jason quietly excused himself to the lounge, leaving Hannah and Kayla alone together.

"I brought us all kinds of fun things to play with Lexi my dear", Kayla said as she slowly unzipped the purple duffel bag she had brought along for the date. She began to pull out vibrators of various shapes and sizes, a few different dildos, a strap-on, a large bottle of toy friendly lubricant, and even a few butt plugs. She laid each item neatly on the small table that was right beside the bed so that everything was within their reach. Hannah watched with interest and responded to each item as Kayla pulled it out of the bag with various oohhs and aahhs. When she was finished laying the toys out, Kayla walked across the room to where Hannah stood and began kissing her on the mouth passionately and deeply just as they had done earlier at Hannah's apartment. Just like it had been before it was instantly dizzying to Hannah. "So, do you like that?", she asked Hannah pulling away slightly so that she could gaze seductively into her eyes.

"Yes, I do like it. It's pretty nice", Hannah answered with slight bashfulness.

"Well, we should definitely start off with something that is pretty nice", Kayla said with a laugh as she pulled Hannah's jacket off her shoulders and placed it out of the way on the corner of the bed.

"You're not going to take my dress off of me, are you?" Hannah asked in a sarcastic tone.

"Now look who's being the demure one?", Kayla joked while rubbing her hand lightly up Hannah's inner thigh. She then pushed the skirt of Hannah's dress up past her plump ass and looked appreciatively at the lingerie underneath without ever touching her skin.

"So, you don't want to play with me now huh?", Hannah said in slight mock disappointment.

"Well, I thought my sweetie may want to spend a little time with me to get him going", Kayla said gesturing over to the lounge where Jason sat alone. "But you might be lucky enough to have some hands-on fun with me afterwards", Kayla said coyly.

"Can I trust you to keep that promise?", Hannah teased her, raising her eyebrows suggestively. Kayla shrugged with a playful smirk. Jason was accustomed to being the man in charge in most situations. He loved that role and anything else caused him to feel anxiousness, so Kayla wanted to take the time to make sure he felt that he was the one calling the shots. She walked over to him with the lace of her thigh-high stockings showing just beneath her dress, and as she had expected he would do, he told her he would rather spend time with her after he got to watch the two ladies have their fun, and that he had really been looking forward to his private show, so Kayla returned to Hannah with an eager smile.

"You're in luck, I guess he wants his show first after all", Kayla said looking as if she were a feline about to pounce on Hannah. Hannah was nearly shaking with nervousness, but so far, she had hidden it well. She decided to calm her nerves by taking control of the situation, so before Kayla could make the first move, Hannah stopped her by grabbing Hannah by the arm and leaning in close to her, placing her lips right above Kayla's ear.

"I want to please you first", she whispered despite her nervousness. She carefully unzipped Kayla's dress, letting it fall straight to the hardwood floor. "It's the least I can do for the girl who got me out of my terrible funk", Hannah said with a wink. The expression on Kayla's face showed her surprise and delightedness at Hannah's unexpectedly bold behavior. Hannah then started to finger Kayla's pussy, delighting in the strong and sweet smell of her desire. "It's not going to take very long sweetie", Hannah promised her, while looking into her eyes.

"I suppose it isn't like you want me to, I'm sure", Kayla said.

"Is that so?" Hannah asked expectantly as she pulled her fingers out and began to lightly flick her fingertips across Kayla's swollen clit.

"It sure looks that way", Kayla said with a giggle.

As Hannah continued to play with Kayla's clit, Kayla moaned and occasionally jerked slightly. She took her hand and softly rubbed it lightly up and down Hannah's thighs and arms, as Kayla started to moan in pleasure. Hannah then began to rub her fingers between Kayla's labia lips, as she parted them and inserted a finger back inside Kayla's wet ready pussy.

"Oh baby, that feels so good", Kayla moaned, enticing Hannah into inserting a second finger inside Kayla's waiting pussy. She began to rapidly finger fuck Kayla with just the two fingers as she kissed her passionately on the lips.

"I think I'm ready", Hannah said to Kayla with a sexy confident smile.

"For what?" Kayla asked coyly, looking into Hannah's bright eyes.

"For you to take me, right here, right now!", Hannah said in a whisper.

"I hope you are ready", Kayla said seductively. Then she suddenly pushed Hannah down hard on the bed and climbed on top of her pinning her down. She grabbed the bottom of Hannah's dress and pulled it over her head and threw it across the room. Together they looked like a montage of good and evil. They had on matching bra and panty sets, each had a garter belt and stockings that went with it as well. Hannah's was white, and Kayla's was deep red. Behind the glass of one of the small windows, Jason was watching as he began to slowly stroke his own cock. Kayla fastened the strap-on tightly around herself and then carefully selected the dildo she wanted to use with it. As she rubbed lubricant on the one that she had decided to use, she kept her eyes intensely locked with Hannah's.

"Oh fuck!", Hannah cried out with pleasure as Kayla thrust her hips forward pushing the dildo deep into Hannah's pussy. Kayla pulled back and thrusted her hips forward again, making Hannah moan, then she grabbed a handful of Hannah's hair and did it a few more times. Hannah reacted more intensely with each thrust.

"Do you like it when I fuck you?", Kayla asked. Hannah nodded to let Kayla know she liked it. Kayla smiled down at her with a handful of Kayla's hair still in her hand. Kayla leaned back, pulled her panties to the side, and forced Hannah to taste her wet pussy.

"Taste it", Kayla demanded, and Hannah obediently extended her tongue and began licking Kayla's pussy tentatively at first and then slowly speeding up. Before long, Hannah had begun licking it hungrily and Kayla leaned back in pleasure and moaned, nearly closing her eyes. Hannah reached to the table and grabbed the first vibrator that caught her eye. She felt it begin to buzz in her hand when she pushed the first button she saw. She pressed it firmly against Kayla's swollen clitoris. Kayla began bucking her hips forward violently and shaking involuntarily and then suddenly she was sent completely over the edge and she began to gush cum from her tight pussy. Hannah caught some of Kayla's sweet juices in her mouth and spit the cum into Kayla's open mouth, then shoving her tongue into her mouth behind it. When Kayla was done coming, she lay there panting as she regained her composure.

"Is that all you got?", Hannah said challenging Kayla. Kayla was suddenly motivated, and she bolted upright and pushed Kayla down onto her hands and knees. She firmly gripped Hannah's soft and perky tits and began plowing into her young tight little hole. She grabbed a small butt plug from the table and eased it into Hannah's ass as she fucked her pussy. The resulting sensation was almost too intense. Hannah began to moan louder and louder till they had nearly become screams. Hannah screamed out one final time as she experienced the most intense pleasure of her entire life. She began to squirt relentlessly, soaking the bed they were on in the process. The sight of this nearly caused Jason to come. He sat stroking his penis as he watched the beautiful ladies, he had hired to give him a show. They were definitely giving him a good one.

The girls collapsed in a hot, wet, pile panting and both in a daze. They were stunned at what had just happened between them. That was not anything like what they had planned. It was not even comparable to the pornography videos from which they had watched for inspiration. Their sexual chemistry paved the way for this to become the hot mess it now was. Neither of the ladies were mad though. Kayla was just hoping that Jason did not get to upset about the bedding they had just soaked. She silently hoped that he had a mattress cover on this thing.

"Oh yes", Jason said as he replayed what had just happened with his imagination. He was remarkably close to coming. Suddenly both girls appeared in the doorway. He let then know he was close to coming so that they were not surprised or caught off guard if it happened. He was pleasantly surprised when both ladies dropped to their knees in front of him ready to take his cum. The sight of them waiting for it sent him over the edge. It was a record-breaking sized load. There was plenty for both of the women to get a cum facial. He loved how they looked with his jizz on their faces. He appreciated the sight for just a moment before giving them each a hand towel to clean their faces with.

Tantric Discovery (Tantra Story)

Hannah and Kayla got themselves cleaned up, dressed, and ready to go. Kayla had planned to take Hannah back to her apartment, and then come right back to Jason's house for a private date. Hannah had another scheduled appointment with Daryl, who had been her first ever client, later that evening. Hannah was in a bit of a hurry to get home so that she had time to shower and do everything else it takes to get herself ready for another date. She grabbed the envelope, which was thick with cash, that Jason had left sitting in the foyer with her escort name, Lexi written across it in red ink. On the drive home they excitedly recapped the events that had just taken place and ranted about how well it had gone. They highlighted all their favorite parts and agreed to get together to celebrate later. Kayla even suggested that they post an ad for a two-girl show and start doing doubles as often as clients come seeking. Upon arriving home, she said bye as she hugged Kayla, and then ran straight to her apartment and to the shower. She was too limited on time to eat or do anything else besides get ready, so she rushed through her shower, rubbing the sudsy loofah across her entire body as quickly as possible and leaning around the water to avoid wetting her hair as much as she could. When she got out, she immediately turned on the blow dryer and dried the parts of her hair that got splashed with the water so that her hair would not become frizzy. She had to clean the streaks of eyeliner from her face which she accidently caused when she rubbed her face with her wet soapy hands. She then redid her make-up, sprayed some perfume all over herself and then went to her room to put on some lingerie. She barely had time to get some music going when she heard the anticipated knock at the door. She peeked out the small peephole and saw Daryl standing there patiently. She opened the door and invited him inside hiding her mostly naked body behind the door in case someone was to walk down the hallway.

"Hello beautiful", he said as he looked at her in appreciation at the strappy black teddy and fishnet stockings she had on.

"Hey babe, thank you", she said back to him with a sweet smile. "How are you today?", she asked him with bubbliness in her voice.

"Oh, I'm doing well", he said back to her cheerfully. When he had first reached out to her to set up a time to come see her again, he had mentioned wanting to try something new with her this time. She asked what it was, but he said he would prefer to discuss that in person if that was alright with her, and she said it was. Daryl seemed like a pretty normal and respectful guy so she doubted his request would be anything so strange that she would feel too uncomfortable to go through with it.

"So, what was it that you wanted to try?", she asked him curiously as she adjusted one of the straps on her teddy in the full-length mirror.

"Tantra", he responded plainly. Hannah just looked back at him with her head slightly tilted to the side and a confused look on her face.

"I'm not sure what that is", Hannah admitted. Daryl began to explain it to her. He said it was like a cross between meditation and sex, and that they would be having sex in different positions with the goal of creating a deep intimate connection between them, while reaching some sort of spiritual enlightenment. Hannah thought it sounded interesting and fun, she liked the idea of combining spirituality and sex. Hannah tried to imagine what the positions would be like as she told Daryl that she would be happy to have this experience with him. She imagined something along the lines of yoga and began to feel a little intimidated by this idea, but it was not too crazy of a request, so she agreed to give it a try. Daryl paid her for several hours of her time because he wanted ti to ensure that they had the time needed to fully experience Tantric sex. He was not particularly familiar with exactly how it was done either, so they had to do a Google search to search for some inspiration and guidance. They learned that the practice usually involved getting to know their own bodies as well as partner's body. According to the research they had done, they would have the best experience if they took the time to get familiar with each other's body prior to getting started, so they decided to begin by exchanging full-body massages.

"Ladies go first of course", Daryl said as he gestured for Hannah to lie down on the bed in front of where he was sitting. She grabbed a jar of coconut oil from her dresser as she slowly lowered herself onto the bed facing downwards. Hannah had been abnormally sore and tense lately and knew she was probably in dire need of a proper massage, but she honestly doubted Daryl was going to be able to really provide that. Her seemed very clumsy and awkward in the way he carried himself, and massages sometimes required grace and sureness in your movements, so she doubted he had the finesse that would be required of a professional masseuse. When he first gripped the back of her neck, she was impressed by how firm and steady his hands felt against the muscles as they began to work the soreness out of her neck. She felt him unzip the back of her teddy completely and he laid both sides of it open on the bed and out of his way. He worked his way slowly but firmly down her body as he let the path his hands took be guided by the natural grooves and curves of her body. She groaned in pleasure when his hands got to that persistently sore spot in the center of her back. She took deep breaths and cleared her mind so that she could focus on enjoying the feeling of his strong hands against her naked body. He massaged all the way down her back, then to her butt cheeks, which he rubbed in a circular motion. She let out a sigh at how amazing it was feeling as he made his way across her thighs and calves. He paid special attention to her feet which he for last.

"Would you please roll onto your back for me now?", he asked in a quietly calming tone. Hannah rolled over, leaving her unzipped teddy lying flat of the bed, and exposing her bare chest and freshly shaved pussy. She looked at him unapologetically and smiled as Daryl marveled at the breath-taking sight of her naked body. He returned his attention to his work and began rubbing the front of her feet with both of his hands, and then he slowly massaged his hands up the front of her body much like how he had done with the back side. He stopped once when he reached her pussy, to lightly brush his fingertips across Hannah's exposed clit for a brief moment before he continued. She felt her pussy begin to tingle and get moist in response to his touch.

"Mmmm", she moaned barely loud enough for Daryl to hear it. When he had finished with her massage, she took her time stretching her muscles out and experiencing the relaxed state her muscles were in as she prepared to swap roles with Daryl. Suddenly she had an idea come to mind. It was something she had been taught by her former sugar daddy.

"Have you ever had a Nuru massage?", Hannah asked Daryl. She was so grateful for the massage he had just given her, and she wanted to make sure Daryl had an equally good experience with his massage in return.

"No, I have not, what's that?", he asked. Hannah explained it in detail and Daryl readily agreed, even mentioning that the idea might also be beneficial to the tantra part of it as well. Hannah prepared by blowing up an air mattress she kept in the hallway closet for guests, then she heated the coconut oil up in her microwave oven, just long enough for it to be melted but being careful to not get it too hot to be used on the skin. Then she gestured for Daryl to follow her into the bathroom to get their skin wet. She turned the shower on and together, they both got in long enough to get enough water on their skin so that the oil would easily spread across their skin and become slippery. Without drying off Daryl laid face-down and naked on the air mattress. Hannah grabbed the coconut oil from the top of her dresser and poured a generous amount over him, and then she poured some over her own wet and naked body. After nearly emptying the entire jar of oil onto their bodies, he began massaging his neck with her hands as she rubbed her tits against his upper-back and simultaneously used her knees to massage his thighs. Her skin glided across his with ease as she moved the various parts of her body against his. She pressed her tits hard against his back and made a circular motion against his thighs using her knees. Suddenly she flipped over so that her back faced his and turned around so that she was sitting in the crease of his lower-back. Her ass cheeks were sliding back and forth smoothly across his back as she used the heels of her feet to massage his tired and achy calf muscles.

"Does it feel good to you?", she asked Daryl who laid there with his eyes closed and a relaxed smile on his face.

"mmmhmm", he replied, dragging the word out to emphasis how much he was enjoying his Nuru massage. She straddled his butt cheeks between her thick thighs and began clenching them together and letting them spread them open just enough so that her pussy barely touched him. She did this over and over quite a few times, which resulted in her thighs firmly massaging both of his butt cheeks and the outer part of his hips. Once she was sure she had thoroughly rubbed every part of the back of his body with at least one part of hers, she politely requested that he turn over so that she could work on the front half of his body. When he did, she smiled at the sight of his penis standing strong and thick and fully hard. It waved back-and-forth a few times as if it were beckoning for her to come play with it. She ignored the beckoning of his cock at first so that she could focus her attention on massaging the front of his legs with her arms. Her knees rubbed against his arms so that her legs were spread open across his chest, giving him a wonderful view of her pussy. Once his arms were free, he reached between her legs and began lightly flicking his finger against her clit as she continued to slide her oiled-up body over the entire front of his body, leaving only his erect penis unmassaged. Then she took her tits and squeezed them together tightly around his cock. She used her hands to bounce her boobs up and down a few times, giving his dick a good tug. Daryl moaned in appreciation as he admired Hannah's body which was shiny from the coconut oil. Once she had finished with his massage, Daryl suggested the start by practicing the breathing technique. They started by sitting on the floor facing each other. They each placed their hand gently on the other's chest and quietly focused on synchronizing their breathing with their eyed closed. After a while, they both felt ready to begin, so Hannah climbed on top of Daryl's crossed legs and slid her still oiled body against his chest as she slipped her pussy down onto his erect cock slowly. She bounced up and down on his member as his hands explored her body. Suddenly she felt him moving his legs.

"My leg is cramping up a bit", Daryl complained. Then he began to straighten both of his legs out underneath her. As he did, he held Hannah's hips in place on his cock, so that she remained where he wanted her to be as he adjusted his position. He moved one of his hands to her chest and cupped the other behind her back to support her. Then he squeezed one of her boobs in his hand as he used it to push her body backwards so that her head was resting on the floor in between the lower half of his legs. He grabbed her hips and used them to slide her pussy up and down his rock-hard cock. They both moaned together in unison. Hannah reached down and began slowly massaging her clit with her fingertips as Daryl slid her pussy up and down the length of his shaft. He pushed himself up onto his knees and put her legs in the air so that her toes were pointed up at the ceiling. She laid on her back as he began thrusting himself deeper into her pussy. She wanted to watch him fucking her, so she pushed herself up so that she was propped up on her elbows. She looked down at her pussy, enjoying the view of his cock going in and out of her tight tiny hole. They both could feel their orgasms beginning to build, and Daryl began to thrust his hips forward harder and faster, slamming himself hard into her pussy. Hannah's eyes rolled back as an orgasm began to crash over her knocking her back like an ocean's wave. Her orgasm was intensified by Daryl's cum, as it began to fill her pussy with a huge load of his hot cum. She thrusted her hips upward momentarily allowing his cock to get even deeper inside of her as they both enjoyed their shared orgasm. As they finished, they both began to relax their bodies feeling completely satisfied.

"Oh, that was amazing. Thank you, babe,", Daryl said as he carefully pulled his cock out of her. Hannah found herself in a bit of a daze from the spectacular orgasm she had just experienced. She decided that she was really impressed by Daryl's performance. She certainly did not expect him to have her legs trembling the way they were. She noticed he seemed to have enjoyed it as much as she had, and she wondered if they had experienced the same levels of intensity. Daryl had only taken up two of the three hours that he had paid for at the beginning of their time together, yet he still left her a forty-dollar tip. As soon as he left, she got out the envelope she had got from Jason and combined it with the cash Daryl had given her. She nearly gasped when she realized that she had made nearly a thousand dollars in a single day.

She thought about how grateful she was to Kayla for teaching her how to earn this kind of money, then she wondered what Kayla was doing so she sent her a text asking her if she was done at Jason's. While she waited for a response an idea about how to repay Kayla for her help came to her suddenly and she could not wait for Kayla to respond so she could tell her all about it. It took Kayla about an hour to respond to Hannah's message, in her response she informed Hannah that she was done at Jason's. Hannah responded by simply telling her to come over as soon as she could and that she had some big news. Within an hour Kayla was banging on the door of Hannah's apartment, curious to know what was going on. When Hannah opened it, she was grinning ear-to ear and hardly able to contain herself.

"Hey what's up?", Kayla asked, curious about Hannah's giddy behavior.

"I was thinking", Hannah began excitedly, "I have an extra bedroom here and I get lonely being here by myself all the time. I was going to ask if you wanted to take the extra bedroom?". Kayla looked a little shocked at first then she smiled back at Hannah with a playful expression.

"I know I'm good, but we only slept together once and you're asking me to move in?", she asked with a smirk as she winked at her friend. Hannah rolled her eyes and laughed along with Kayla. "I mean, I would love to", Kayla finally said with a grateful smile. Hannah began on a rant about how much easier it would be for them to work together, and how much fun they would have. Kayla agreed when she pointed out that splitting the apartment's rent would be much cheaper than having to pay for a hotel every day. They talked about it for a couple hours and went over how things would work and how they would split bills and chores. Hannah told her that she was welcome to sleep on the couch tonight and they could go get her a bed tomorrow if she wanted. Kayla agreed but she had to return to the hotel to get her things, so Hannah decided to ride along with her. She had never been to the hotel Kayla stayed at and she wondered why she had never been invited over, so she had been curious to see what it was like for a while now.

Hannah was shocked and a little nervous by the scene before her when they pulled up to the place her friend had been staying. It was in a part of town she had never been to. The rundown looking motel, which was across from the airport, was befittingly called The Airport Inn. There were plastic chairs outside of many of the rooms where people sat with forty-ounce beers or cigarettes or both in their hands. It felt dangerous to Hannah, and it made her feel even better about her decision to ask Kayla to move in. Kayla's room was on the second floor. She instructed Hannah to stay in the car while she ran up and grabbed her things and said bye to a couple of friends. Hannah did as she was told and was grateful when Hannah locked her in the car. Just a few minutes later Kayla was back in the car and they were on the way to the safety of the apartment. Hannah decided not to say anything about the conditions at the hotel because she did not want to offend Kayla or say anything to hurt her feelings. When they got back Hannah poured them each a strong drink and they piled up in Hannah's bed to watch a funny movie.

The following morning Hannah got out of bed. Kayla was still sleeping peacefully so Hannah decided to let her be. It was almost two in the afternoon when she finally made her way out of bed. At Hannah's request they got ready and made their way to the furniture store to get a bed for Kayla's room. They did not spend but a few minutes inside the small furniture store Kayla decided to check out. She was very quick to pick one of the least expensive bed frames the place had in stock. The salesman had barely managed to talk her into getting a mattress that was slightly better than their least expensive option. After taking the money and adding it to the cash register, he scheduled for the bed to be delivered directly to the apartment the following day since it was not going to fit in Kayla's small car. On their way back to the apartment they stopped and got some Chinese food takeout. Kayla and Hannah discussed that they would keep a shared schedule so they could schedule their appointments to see clients around each other. Kayla often went to her client's homes to see them so that made the scheduling much more convenient for them both. Everything seemed to work out perfectly and the girls were both feeling good about their decision to move in together.

"What are you doing up so early?", Hannah asked Kayla groggily as Kayla hurriedly was getting herself ready for something. Hannah saw that she was wearing a skirt that went past her knees which was something she had never seen before.

"I'm getting ready for church", she said hurriedly as she finished throwing her hair into a neat ponytail.

"Church?", Hannah asked clearly confused.

"Every Sunday", Kayla clipped back. Hannah watched silently as Kayla finished getting ready and rushed out the door. She had heard Kayla say some religious things before, but she still did not think she was the type to go to church every Sunday. Hannah was quite surprised by this new information, but she decided that it was probably a good thing. Hannah was not a believer herself, but she appreciated how it drove people to have strong morals and to treat others well. When Kayla returned a few hours later Hannah had decided to go on without mentioning it. She was somewhat curious about what inspired her friend to go to church, but she figured her friend would tell her when and if she felt like it. The bed was delivered that afternoon and the girls set it up together. The instructions were a little confusing, but they had fun figuring it out together. When it was done Hannah pushed the extra nightstand that she had into Kayla's room so that she had a couple drawers for her socks and underwear, and anything else she could not hang up.

"Hey, I might have a client over tomorrow if you don't already have plans", Kayla said once they had finished getting the bed together.

"Sure, okay. Just be sure to update the schedule on your phone. It will automatically block out any times that I have plans", Hannah reminded her. Kayla asked for Hannah's help doing that and they blocked out the time that her client was wanting to come by.

A special request (Anal Story)

"Could I ask you something? It's kind of embarrassing but I need to ask", Hannah said looking timidly at Kayla. Kayla reminded her that they were close enough that most things should not be embarrassing to talk about. She used their experience at Jason's house as an example to prove her point. Hannah asked if Kayla had ever done anal for a client. She told her that she had a potential client who was offering a pretty large sum of cash for it, and Hannah felt tempted.

"Yes, I actually do pretty regularly", she answered, "Have you ever done it at all?". Hannah said she had a boyfriend who had been really into it her first year of college, so she had done it plenty of times, she just did not know if it was a common request or if it was okay to agree to do something like that with a client, the potential mess she pointed out as an example. Kayla explained that Hannah could do it, but she would probably want to take some measures to prevent any embarrassing incidents. She took Hannah to the adult store and helped her get the necessary supplies. When they got back to the apartment Hannah texted her client to set up a time. He seemed incredibly eager to make it happen and decided to schedule it for the following day. Hannah was nervous but wanted to get it done with, so she agreed to it despite it being so soon. She exchanged a few photos with the client, who's name was Tyler, and was surprised to find that he was a very good-looking guy. He looked young, maybe in his late twenties at most, and he had dirty blonde hair and bright blue eyes. She was not sure if that increased or decreased her level of nervousness, but she was sure that it would make the whole thing a little more enjoyable. The following morning Hannah got things in her room so that she would not have to leave it for a couple hours while Kayla took her date. Kayla assured her that this was a regular client and would be no trouble, and Hannah responded by telling her not to worry about it.

"I'm not worried at all, I trust you", she told Kayla with a confident smile as she closed her bedroom door. Kayla sat down and put the television on. She heard a knock not long after and Kayla opened the front door and invited the client in. By the way he talked, she figured this was a client from the motel Kayla had been staying at. This made Hannah nervous, but she told herself that she needed to trust Kayla and decided that she would not say anything or make a fuss about it unless it became a real issue. Once they had went to Kayla's room. She did not hear anything else until Kayla and her client said bye and she walked him out, but about ten minutes before the date ended, she did begin to smell the unrecognizable scent of marijuana seeping into her room. Hannah did not want to mess up Kayla's date so she decided to talk to her about it once he was gone, but she could swear she remembered telling Kayla that they were not allowed to smoke in the apartment and that it could get them kicked out if they were caught. So, she sat there, alone in her room and the more and the longer she smelled the stink of the weed, the more upset she started feeling at Kayla's disregard for the rules.

"What in the world was that?", Hannah asked as soon as she opened her door. Kayla looked at her with a confused expression and asked what Hannah was talking about.

"It reeks of weed in here", Hannah said as she crossed her arms and eyed Kayla with a stern expression. Kayla acted as if she were surprised that Hannah was upset about her smoking weed inside the apartment.

"I don't remember us talking about not smoking weed in here but it won't happen again", Kayla said with a scowl. Hannah reminded her of the no smoking conversation, to which Kayla said she assumed that Hannah had been referring to cigarettes.

"Any kind of smoke", Hannah clarified still a little annoyed. Kayla apologized and assured Hannah that it would not happen again, so Hannah decided to let it go and went back to her room to cool off and start getting ready for her upcoming date. Once she felt totally calm again, she asked Kayla for one more explanation on how to use the supplies they had gotten from the adult store the day before. Kayla gave her a final detailed explanation and Hannah listened intently and mentally repeated each instruction back to herself so that she remembered every detail. When she was done getting ready, she still had at least thirty minutes before Tyler was supposed to arrive, so she decided to hang out with Kayla in the meantime. Hannah apologized for getting so upset about smelling the weed.

"That's okay, I get it", Kayla said before apologizing for not initially understanding what Hannah had meant when they talked about smoking in the apartment. They sat and talked until a few minutes before Hannah's new client was set to arrive. She got up to check herself in the mirror one last time before he got there. The incoming call she had been expecting finally came through. When she answered it, a smooth deep voice came through the line asking her where he should park. She stood at the window until she saw him get out of the car. Hannah quickly identified him as the guy from the photo and he certainly did not disappoint. He was tall but not too tall, and he was in shape too. When he made it to the door Hannah already had it cracked ready to welcome him inside. As he walked through the door, she could not help but notice the large bulge in the front of his khaki pants. He was clearly very well endowed, which made Hannah feel suddenly nervous about what was about to happen. She managed to bring her attention up to his face.

"Hey babe, come on back to my room", she said keeping a straight face. He smiled and nodded and followed her back to her bedroom. Once inside he immediately removed his shoes. Hannah stripped down to the lingerie she had on underneath her clothes. She could hear him behind her following her lead and stripping off his pants and shirts. She turned around and without realizing how close behind her he was she nearly ran into him.

"Woah", she said looking down. She was not necessarily saying that because she had nearly ran into him. It was because she now could see exactly how well-endowed he was now that he had nothing left on but his boxers. When he followed her gaze to his member he looked at her apologetically.

"I probably should have mentioned...", he said trailing off, unsure of how to finish his sentence. Hannah felt a little bad for him, clearly, he got this reaction quite often.

"No, it's fine, or it should be", Hannah said with an unmistakable doubt in her voice.

"You look stunning", he offered as if it would help the situation.

"Thank you", Hannah said as she made her way over to him. He touched her waist, looking at her as if wondering if this were okay. "I have a few butt plugs", she said without making eye contact with him, "do you suppose we could start with those and work our way up to it".

"Of course,", he said looking relieved that she was even willing to try. She grabbed two butt plugs and some anal lubricant from her dresser drawer, the first was a medium sized silicone one with a red heart at the tip, and the other was exceptionally large, it was made of metal and it had a round pink gem on it. She had never used that one. It was too big for her, but she figured now would be the time to get used to it. She bent over in front of him and pushed the smaller one of the two slowly into her butt. She made a face when the thickest part of it entered, it caught her off guard, but she found it was surprisingly comfortable. He grabbed the end that stuck out and moved it around and she arched her back out in

81

response to the feeling of him pushing it deeper into her ass. "Do you think you can take the larger one?", he asked eagerly.

"I think so", she responded questioningly. She gasped as he pulled the smaller one out of her ass. She felt the pressure from the larger one against her hole within moments. She let out a whimper as it began to push into her bottom. The girth of it almost made her lose her balance, but she braced herself against her bed post and managed to remain standing.

"Just relax", he told her after several minutes of her struggling with it.

"I'm trying", she snapped, but in reality, she was really enjoying herself.

"Relax and stay put", he firmly instructed as he applied some more lubricant around the plug, "It'll hurt a little bit, but I won't let you fall". She quickly acquiesced, but she made sure not to let the plug end of it out. The larger one fit much more comfortably now, but the pressure of it resting inside her made her gulp down a few quick breaths. She was going to try to do this, so she tried not to freak out. "Don't move, alright?", he asked.

"I won't", she grumbled, but she did relax her body as the rest of it slid in. After several minutes, she could feel the pressure subside a little as it settled into place.

"Good. Now that it is all the way in, I'm going to move it around a bit before taking it out.", he informed her. She did not answer. She simply moved her hips back slightly, so that it pushed as far into her as it could go. He pushed her further into the bed as he applied a bit more pressure. She grunted out a sigh when she felt the tip go deep into her bottom. She felt it begin to stretch her asshole as he wriggled it around inside of her. Once he was satisfied, she began to feel the pressure of him pulling on the butt plug. She could not help but to clench her ass tightly holding it inside of her. "Relax", he reminded her gently. She refocused her mind and forced her body to relax so he could get the huge butt plug out of her tight little asshole. She felt it slowly being pulled out of her. He applied some more lubricant around the edge of it to help it along before he kept pulling. After a moment of an intense feeling that made her hold her breath, she felt it pop out and she sighed as she relaxed herself on the bed.

"Okay", she sighed, "I think I'm ready". Her heart began to pound as he pressed his huge cock against her asshole.

"You are ready for this?", he asked.

"Uh-huh", she responded, "I'm still a bit nervous. I've never taken a cock this big in my ass, so please try to take it easy on me", she requested, as she reached up to run her fingers through her hair, pushing it out of her face as she waited for his big cock to make its way into her ass.

"Okay baby, I'll try not to hurt you too bad.", he said, smiling at her before pushing his massive cock into her tight asshole. He could feel her tight ring stretch to accommodate his shaft and when the head broke past her sphincter, he froze. "It's still a bit tight, I think we

83

need to get it a bit looser.", he stated, before slowly pushing it in further. He did not want to get too aggressive with her asshole just yet, since he did not want to end up having to stop if he caused her too much pain. After pushing his cock deeper and further into her until she felt it lodge against her sphincter muscle, he let out a loud groan and began to pump his cock in and out of her slowly.

"Oh shit... that is the tightest ass I've ever had.", he exclaimed, continuing to pump his cock into her, "damn, it feels so good". He began to get increase his pace with each of his strokes and he had to wrap his hands under her legs and ass to keep her from rising and hitting her head against the headboard. He continued to pump his cock in and out of her as she began to pant and moan. He started to fuck her faster, punching her small but firm little butt as hard as he could as he slammed into her tight asshole.

"Oh god, I'm gonna come!", he told her in between rapid thrusts.

"Ughh. Oh god, yeah!", she responded with a moan, reaching up and grabbing his balls in both hands as his cock pumped in and out of her tiny butt hole.

"Yeah, yeah, yeah! Give me that ass bitch!", he encouraged, thrusting harder as he reached his peak. He felt his cock twinge as he felt the first blast of cum shoot into her small asshole.

"Ooooooohhhhhhhhhhhhhhhhh", she moaned in pleasure, as she squeezed his dick with her ass. The thought of his massive cock filling up her tiny ass with his cum was too much for him and he came several more times filling her little butt up with his spunk. He gently pulled his dick out of her ass and her little butt hole slowly opened up and then closed again. He slid his hands up her little ass to hold on to her ass cheeks to make sure his cum remained inside of her.

"Yeah... that was good.", he said, laughing. He started to grab his boxers to slide them back on and she slowly began getting dressed too. "Can I come back and see you sometime?", he asked as he sat a white envelope on her dresser. She smiled at him flirtatiously and said he could, and he knew that she had enjoyed it as much as he had.

"Thank you, hopefully I'll see you again soon", she said politely and cheerfully as she showed him out. She closed and locked the door behind him and went straight back to her room as the day's events sunk in. She had an uncomfortable feeling of guilt as she often did after seeing most of the clients. She had felt it for the first time after she had first met Daryl and sucked him off. She felt it again when she had her first lesbian experience with Kayla at Jason's house. She even felt it when Kayla would explain to her how her dates went and describe the events that took place. She was not sure what made her feel this way, and despite trying, she could not make sense of it. She did not think she had any hidden moral issues with what she was doing. She did not feel she was hurting anyone by escorting. In fact, most of the time she felt empowered by it. It is her body, and she was proud to be resourceful enough to use it to provide for herself. She also felt it might even be able to be considered a good deed because she brought joy to these men, many of which seemed to need it badly. She sat alone in her room and contemplated her reasons for feeling so down after most of her dates but came to no conclusion. Suddenly she heard a light tap at her bedroom door.

"Are you awake Hannah?", Kayla called in from the hallway in what was barely more than a whisper. Hannah felt instantly annoyed by the interruption and had almost snapped at Kayla for invading her privacy. She barely caught herself just in time knowing that Kayla was not trying to do that at all.

"I'm up", she called back through the door, "Just having a bit of a moment". Kayla kindly asked her if she thought some food might help improve her mood. Hannah realized she had not eaten at all that day and she felt her stomach grumble angrily at the mere thought of food. Hannah told her friend that she was starving, and she would be out in just a moment so they could figure out what to do for dinner.

"Alright", Kayla responded. Hannah could hear the concern in her friend's voice, but she brushed it off for now figuring that Kayla would see her move improve when they got food and it would resolve itself. She could not help but to wonder if she just was not cut out to be an escort. The feeling of despair was intense and on the way to the restaurant they had chosen to eat at, she broke down and told Kayla all about how she had been feeling. Kayla listened and nodded with an understanding but sad expression that made Hannah wonder if she had experienced the same thing at some point. Kayla suggested that Hannah go to church with her the following Sunday. She said being involved in something like that, something that is about the greater good, helped her feel a sense of normalcy and strengthened her morals. Hannah felt very doubtful that church would be the solution to her problems, but she reluctantly agreed to go after Kayla had pushed a few times, insisting that it could not hurt to try it. Kayla found an outfit that was church appropriate and laid it out when she got home. She was surprised that she had found something appropriate. She asked Kayla if she could help remind her to iron the wrinkles out of it the night before they go, and shortly after both girls went to their own rooms.

Over the next few days both girls saw quite a few clients. Hannah began to hope that church would in fact offer her some sort of reprieve from her turmoil. She was growing tired of having to deal with this sinking feeling of depression each time she worked. Even Kayla could see how badly it was impacting Hannah, and she tried to help however she could, but her every effort only seemed to make the problem worse. Hannah had begun to become short-tempered and snappy with her, and more and more she stopped trying to help and began avoiding Hannah instead. On Saturday night Kayla was surprised to hear that Hannah was still planning to accompany her to church. Kayla explained a few important things about Catholic churches to Hannah and reminded her to iron her dress as she had requested. When they were both ready, they bid one another a good night, and each went to their rooms and went to bed.

"Hannah, it's time to get up", Kayla called sweetly through the door. Hannah sat upright wondering why she was being woken up, then she remembered that she was supposed to be going along with Kayla to church today.

"Okay, I'm up", she called back to Kayla. Hannah felt nervous and considered backing out, but something inside her was urging her to go, and she could not ignore it. Maybe it was self-loathing or morbid curiosity, but regardless, Hannah got herself ready as quickly as possible and made herself a quick breakfast before her and Kayla headed out the door. When they arrived, Hannah noticed that the outside of the church was breath-takingly pretty. It was a huge brick building, of which some parts of were as high as four stories. One of the largest towers had an enormous clock with roman numerals, and most of the windows had unique shapes that made the place look incredibly old, and there were some statures which Hannah found to be quite creepy, and she had avoided walking near them. It all looked like something that belonged in Europe. The inside of the church was somehow even prettier than the outside. Hannah looked in awe at the stained-glass windows which depicted incredibly detailed images and scenes that were famously described in the bible. There were beautiful and elegant gold arches lining every doorway in sight, and the warm lighting casted some remarkable shadows that made the place look magical. They slid their way quietly into an empty pew and waited patiently for the church service to start as everyone else took their seats.

Hannah sat and listened intently throughout the entire service, which seemed to last for hours, she stood when everyone else did, put a generous sum of money in the collections plate when it came around to her, and she ate the bread and wine that had been distributed during the service. Kayla looked over at her with a curious expression periodically and silently wondered what she was thinking. Hannah just sat quietly taking it all in. After the service she followed close behind Kayla, who spoke to a few people she knew briefly, and she returned any greeting that had been extended to her. She then followed Kayla over to the confessional box.

"Do you want to go first?", she asked Hannah gesturing to the box.

"No, after you", Hannah replied shaking her head. When Kayla was done, Hannah went into the box and sat down as her heart pounded.

"I don't know how to do this", she confessed to the mysterious figure she could barely make out sitting on the other side of the box. She heard a chuckle from the other side and felt a little embarrassed, but when he spoke again her embarrassment subsided because of the kindness and wisdom she could hear in the man's voice.

"That's quite alright", he said with a smile that she could almost hear. Then he walked her through the steps of confessing patiently and with a tone that made her feel safe and loved. Hannah was not sure why, but she felt so comfortable that she openly admitted everything without holding back. She found it strange because she was normally so reserved. She felt relieved when she was done and out of the box. She wondered how much time she had spent in there. She walked out and her and Kayla went to the car in a peaceful silence. She still did not consider herself a religious person, but she had to admit that it had felt good to confess all her wrongdoings. She felt refreshed and renewed as she returned home with Kayla.

"What did you think?", Kayla asked probingly.

"I don't know", Hannah replied with genuine cluelessness, "I still don't buy into it, but it felt strangely refreshing regardless". Kayla asked if she wanted to keep going back, and Kayla responded by saying that she probably would not go back anytime soon. Kayla was a little disappointed that Hannah did not want to keep going but she decided to not push the issue because she feared it would drive a wedge between them. Thankfully, Hannah's attitude seemed to improve greatly over the next few days. She still had the same uncomfortable feeling after seeing her clients, but she was able to handle it better now. She had gotten caught up and even ahead on her rent. It was especially easy with Kayla's help. The two girls even spent an evening bonding over some drinks, a movie, and conversation like they did when Kayla had first moved in. Everything felt nice and relaxed around the house again. This was a great relief to Kayla who had started to wonder how much longer she was going to have a place to stay. She had a client who had made a request some time back, but Kayla did not feel comfortable asking Hannah about it. With everything seemingly getting back to normal she began to consider asking Hannah about her client's inquiry.

The More the Merrier
(Gangbang Story)

"Hannah, can you come in here for a second? I wanted to ask you a question", Kayla called loudly from her room. Moments later the door to Kayla's room swung open. Hannah stood there with a bottle of wine in her hand.

"What's up? Want some?", she asked gesturing to the bottle in her hand.

"You know I do", Kayla replied enthusiastically. Hannah ran to the kitchen to pour two glasses of the wine. She returned with the glasses and the rest of the bottle in tow. She plopped down on the bed beside Kayla.

"You wanted to ask me something?", she reminded Kayla. Kayla looked at Hannah with a serious expression and told her she had a client who was wanting to see them both. Hannah looked at Kayla with a quizzical expression. "You made it sound like it was going to be something bigger than that", she questioned.

"Oh, it is", Kayla insisted. "The client has a few friends who want to participate as well", she murmured quietly almost hoping that Hannah had not heard her.

"What?", Hannah exclaimed, "Not way I'm doing that, how many friends?". Kayla said that her client was wanting for three of his friends to participate. Hannah thought this over and came to the conclusion that with four guys and two of them, it would not be that hard to handle. It should be like having a threesome basically. "How much?", Hannah queried, doubting they would be paying enough. Kayla leaned in close and whispered to her that they would be getting two thousand each. Kayla's mouth fell open and her eyes went wide. She smiled at Kayla excitedly.

"So, you're in?", Kayla implored.

"Oh, I'm in", Hannah replied with a grin. They both began screaming excitedly at the prospect of making four thousand dollars in just a couple hours. Hannah leaned over Kayla's shoulder as she texted a client whose name was Alfie. They both kept glancing at her phone as the drank wine and enthusiastically chatted about the ordeal.

"Oh my god, I got a message", Kayla screamed. Hannah leaned in close to see what it said. He was wanting to set it up for Friday, in the early afternoon or evening. Both girls had open schedules on Friday, so they were happy to agree. They planned to meet at four in the evening at a really nice hotel. Hannah was happy they were getting a room because she was not sure about having that many people in the apartment at once. They spent the remainder of the night celebrating and after finishing the wine off and putting dents in two fresh bottles of liquor, they both got quite drunk. They passed out together in Kayla's bed as they were playing a funny card game. They both had a great night and had begun feeling like things were finally getting back to normal between them.

Kayla woke up and looked around Kayla's room groggily. There was a card stuck to her face and her back was hurting badly from sleeping on Kayla's shitty mattress. She began to recall the events that took place the night before. A pit formed in her stomach when she remembered what she had agreed to. The idea of participating in a gangbang made her feel sick to her stomach. She got out of the bed and crept to her room and tried to watch some television to distract herself. After over an hour of watching the television, she realized that she was very thirsty. She made her way to the kitchen to get herself something to drink. She was pouring some apple juice into a glass when she suddenly was startled by someone behind her.

"Is there any coffee made yet", Kayla muttered.

"Fuck!", Hannah screamed angrily, "Don't fucking sneak up o n me like that. Kayla shrunk back, shocked by Hannah's aggressive response.

"I'm sorry", Kayla whispered as she tried to remember if she had done something to upset Hannah. She could not remember if she had but she was obnoxiously drunk last night, so she did not really know. "Did I do something wrong?", she asked.

"Just don't sneak up on me like that anymore", Hannah barked. The rest of the next few days continued on this way. Kayla wondered what had caused Hannah's sudden change. She tried to avoid her as much as she possibly could, and she returned to wondering if she would need to get a new place soon. Friday rolled around before they knew it. Kayla almost dreaded the day because she knew it meant interacting with Hannah more. They began getting ready around one in the afternoon. They picked some lingerie that matched well and threw some cute outfits on over the lingerie. Alfie texted her the address of the hotel. She looked it up and saw it was one of the nicest hotels in town. She went to show Hannah hoping this might bring her out of her funk and get her excited.

"Look at this hotel", Kayla began, "Isn't it stunning?". Hannah looked at the picture on Kayla's phone.

"It's nice", she answered without any enthusiasm.

"What is wrong with you?", Kayla blurted. Hannah looked at her for a moment.

"I'm really sorry. I have not been sleeping well at all and it's been putting me in a mood", Hannah whined. She sat down on the edge of Kayla's bed. "I'll get better before the date I promise", she offered. Kayla nodded an agreeance and they finished getting themselves ready in silence. At around three-fifteen they got in Kayla's car and made their way over to the hotel. Alfie sent Kayla the room number once they got to the hotel. The room was up on the twenty-sixth floor of the beautiful and eloquently decorated skyrise hotel. They felt as though they were in the elevator for ages as it stopped to pick people up and to drop others off at different floors of the hotel on their way up. The button with the number twenty-six finally lit up and the elevator made a dinging noise. When the doors opened, they both stepped out of the elevator quickly. They followed the signs on the wall to room two six five nine, Kayla tapped on the door lightly. A stocky man with a big curly brown beard answered the door and greeted them.

"Alfie!", Kayla shouted as she wrapped her arms around the big man. He returned her hug.

"You must be Lexi", he spoke looking at Hannah. Hannah nodded politely and smiled up at him. "Come on in", he added as he gestured them inside. They noticed the three other men sitting in chairs around a computer. All three immediately got up and greeted the girls as Alfie introduced them. The first had short brown hair and glasses, he was clean cut and wore a button up. "This is Brandon", Alfie announced. He tried to offer his hand for them to shake but both gave him a hug instead. The next guy was clearly athletic. His muscles almost ripped through his t-shirt. There was no way he did not lift weights. Alfie introduced him as Calvin. When they hugged him, they could feel the hardness of his entire body. The last guy was thin and tall, he had tattoos covering almost every visible piece of skin on his body and his ears had some huge gauges in them. "Finally, this is Frank", Alfie proclaimed. Hannah noticed the enticing smell of Frank's cologne. Alfie introduced the ladies next, and then Kayla excused herself to the restroom dragging Hannah along. Once inside they stripped down to their lingerie and spritzed themselves with some perfume with pheromones that Kayla had bought them at the adult store.

"We have got this", Kayla assured Hannah. Hannah closed her eyes and breathed deeply for a moment.

"Alright, here we go", Hannah chirped. When they walked back through the door all the men's eyes fell on them and remained locked onto them a each of them examined them both thoroughly. There were practically foaming at the mouth.

"oo, oo, oo", Alfie chirruped, "just because we're an odd group doesn't mean shit". The other men began to nod in agreement as Alfie spoke. "We aren't gonna take it easy on you", Alfie swore. At this point Hannah had already gotten herself completely into character.

"I would be disappointed if you did", she flirted. A couple of the guys chuckled and then Frank walked up to Hannah and grabbed her.

"This is gonna be fun", Frank proclaimed. Frank's breath smelled of vodka. He poured himself another shot and offered one to Hannah. She took it graciously. She threw the shot back and he grabbed the glass from her and sat it on the table. Then he grabbed her wrists and pinned her down on the bed.

"Are you ready slut?", he challenged with a smirk on his face.

"Good question," she replied coolly. Suddenly it was not just Frank who stood over her, Brandon was there too and they both began pawing at her. She whimpered as she felt her tit getting squeezed hard. She could not help it; her pussy became involuntarily wet. Before she knew it Frank was pounding his cock into her tight little pussy, and she was gagging on Brandon's huge cock at the same time.

"Mmmmmm", Kayla moaned as Alfie carefully eased his boner into her tight asshole. Calvin grabbed her by the hair and shoved his dick deep into her mouth.

"Jesus Christ, she's good!", Calvin remarked as she sucked him hard. Alfie wrapped his arms around Kayla's waist and pinned her down with his massive cock between her legs.

"Suck that cock bitch!", Brandon demanded. Hannah looked at Frank and then up at Brandon. Both men looked down on her pitiful body and smiled as they shoved their cocks into her various holes. Frank was thoroughly enjoying fucking Hannah, slowly moving his massive cock in and out of her tight pussy as Bryson leaned over her and sucked on one of her tits. His hard cock was sliding in and out of her gagging mouth like it had been born to be there.

Calvin was licking up and down Kayla's neck. His tongue moved up to her ear lobe and down to her soft tits. The feeling of his tongue on her nipples caused Kayla to squeal with delight. She leaned her head back and closed her eyes as his lips began to work their magic. He began kissing his way down her belly.

"Fuck yeah," Alfie growled as he pounded himself into her. Alfie continued fucking Kayla, grabbing her long dark hair and holding her head back so he could slam himself into her tight pussy as she gagged on Calvin's cock and moaned loudly. Calvin straddled her face and groaned loudly as he fucked it hard. Suddenly cum spurted out of his cock and into Kayla's mouth.

"Fuck yeah!", he called out as he kept pumping his cock in her mouth till all the cum was out. Kayla excused herself to the restroom so she could get a drink and rinse the cum out of her mouth. While she was away all four men advanced on Hannah.

"Can you lick my dick clean bitch?", Calvin asked her.

"Yeah," Hannah replied instantly and took Calvin's huge thick cock in her mouth. Hannah sucked Calvin's cock hard, taking all the cum off of it and licking it all off her lips.

"That's the way," Calvin declared as he pulled his cock from her mouth.

"It's my turn now", Alfie demanded. He grabbed Hannah's hair and forcefully pulled her head back so he could shove his cock into her mouth and go at it. Hannah gagged as his huge cock filled her throat. She gagged again when his balls touched her nose. While Alfie face fucked her Frank was busy ponding his cock into her pussy and Brandon was fucking her tight little ass. Brandon began panting as he used all the force that he could gather to push himself deeper and deeper into her ass.

"I'm gonna cum in your slut hole", Brandon screamed as he pumped himself into her as hard as he could. He let out a loud groan and Hannah began to feel her asshole being filled with his cum. He kept pumping and it kept squirting out in bursts. When he was done, he pulled his cock out gently and patted her on the cheek. "Good job my little slut", he said. Kayla came out of the restroom and Alfie abruptly quit fucking Hannah's mouth and ran to Kayla. He grabbed her by the arm and pulled her over to where Hannah was.

"I wanna see you two fuck each other now", Alfie declared.

"What a great idea', Frank said to Alfie as he pulled his cock out of Hannah. They ordered Kayla to lick Hannah's pussy. Alfie grabbed her by the hair and pulled her down to her knees. She stuck her tongue out and began flicking it against Hannah's clit. Hannah moaned and arched her back. Frank grabbed Hannah by the waist and turned her onto all fours. Alfie shoved Kayla's face into Hannah's wet pussy. Frank grabbed Hannah's ass cheeks and spread them apart to show off her open asshole and the cum that was left inside. Kayla kept licking Hannah's clit until Hannah began to shake and moan. She came hard as Alfie shoved Kayla's face into her pussy.

"Now it's time to please me whore", Alfie said as he pulled Kayla to her feet. He bent her over the back of the couch and pounded his cock into her ass until he came hard into her. As he came in her, Kayla began to cry out as she felt an orgasm overcome her. "Fuck, that pussy is so good", Alfie announced as he emptied the last of his cum in her.

"Fuck me, bitch", Frank yelled as he pulled Hannah back by her hips, slamming her hard into his cock as she remained on all fours in front of him. He kept ramming his cock harder into her swollen pussy. Hannah knew she was going to cum again, she panted and moaned as Frank kept slamming himself into her sore pussy. "Don't worry babe, I'm gonna cum soon", he assured her. He pumped his cock into her a few more times before his huge load emptied into Hannah's pussy. She moaned loudly and pushed herself back onto his cock harder. She moaned and squealed as he emptied every bit of his seed into her. Then she suddenly felt his body relax and she knew he had finished.

"Good girl", he said as he smacked her hard on the bare ass. "You girls sure were a treat", he said as he turned to walk towards the bathroom. The other men all agreed in unison and began giving both girls celebratory slaps on their asses. Hannah went to the bathroom and got herself cleaned up a little and dressed. Kayla came in about halfway through and started getting herself dressed and presentable as well. There was an awkward tension between the two that Kayla could not explain. Hannah seemed upset about something, but Kayla was not sure what it could be. As soon as she finished getting ready Hannah left the bathroom without saying a word to Kayla, and when Kayla came out the guys said that she had already went down to the car. Kayla said goodbye to the guys and followed Hannah down to the car.

"Hey, What's up?", Kayla asked Hannah as she got into the car and started it.

"What do you mean?", Hannah scowled at Kayla.

"Well, you seem pretty upset", she suggested.

"Did you know that all four of them were on me the entire time you spent in the bathroom?", Hannah asked accusingly.

"I am sorry. I started my period unexpectedly and I had to go take care of the situation", Kayla explained.

"Yeah, well that really sucked for me", Hannah said clearly not letting up. Kayla drove them home as they sat in silence. Once there Hannah went straight to her room and shut the door behind her. She took out the envelope the men had given her and counted the money. It was exactly two thousand dollars. She knew she had not been fair about the situation. Kayla could not help it that her body picked the worst possible time to start bleeding. She felt a twinge of guilt underneath the anger but in the end anger won. She was pissed that she had been left to deal with all four of those men alone. On top of that Hannah was feeling the familiar unrest that she felt after seeing a client. She could not handle the intensity of the emotions that bubbled up inside of her. She felt as though she were about to explode with anger. She got up and stormed out of her room. She stomped down the hallway to Kayla's closed door. Hannah pounded on it with her fist a few times before throwing it open.

"I want you to move out immediately", She screamed at Kayla who sat there looking stunned and confused. Hannah did not wait for a response. She slammed the door closed again and stormed out of the apartment. She felt a desperate need to get as far from there as she could. She went walking down the street with no specific destination in mind. There was a small shopping center with a restaurant, an insurance place, and three small stores. She was far from hungry and had no need for any insurance, so she walked right past those two places. The first store was a cute boutique that sold women's clothes. A door chime dinged loudly as she pulled the door open. A lady greeted Hannah as she walked inside, Hannah just nodded in her direction. She walked around the store, quietly examining anything that caught her attention. She filled her arms with things she liked and then piled it on the counter beside the register. The lady had to type the price of each item into the old resister individually. When she was done, she pressed a few more buttons and then looked up at Hannah.

"That'll be two-hundred and sixteen dollars and twenty-seven cents", she said before adding, "I gave you a five percent discount since you are buying so many items". She smiled at Hannah and Hannah pulled the envelope from her pocket as she thanked the lady for the discount. She took three of the one-hundred-dollar bills and threw them on the counter in front of the woman. The lady told Hannah that she had to go to the back to get her change and Hannah just nodded at her. After a few moments, the woman returned with Hannah's change and counted it out for her on the counter. Hannah left the store with three bags full of clothes on her arm. When she got outside, Hannah looked at the second store to see what they sold. It was a home décor place. Through the window she could see an adorable lamp that she thought would look perfect on her bedside table. Hannah went inside and spent almost three hundred more. The third store was a shop that sold baby clothes, which she had no use for, so she walked past it and back to the sidewalk. The bags were starting to feel quite heavy, and Hannah kept having to shift the weight of it. She was thinking about turning around and walking back when she saw the church that her and Kayla had gone to. She decided she would go to the church to sit down for a moment and rest her arms before walking home because her arms sere burning from the weight of the bags. She looked around still in awe of the places beauty as she walked in. It was much emptier than it had been last time. There were a few people praying amongst the pews but not many. Hannah slid into one of the pews and sat her bags down. She stretched her arms out and looked around for a moment before picking up a bible out of the back of the pew in front of her. She opened it and began flipping through it mindlessly. She felt a light tap on her shoulder and looked up to see the priest standing there looking at her.

"You were here with Kayla a couple weeks ago were you not?", she asked her with a friendly smile.

"Um, yeah I was actually", Hannah responded.

"I've known Kayla for quite some time now", he stated before a concerned look came across his face. "Are you okay? I was just sensing that there might be something troubling you", he questioned Hannah.

"I had an argument with Kayla actually, and I went walking, then I bought some things, and they were getting really heavy, so I had to stop to rest", Hannah blurted. She was not sure why she had been so honest and had given so much detail to this man who she hardly knew. She felt immediately embarrassed. He looked at Hannah with a look of understanding.

"Well, I don't want to be a bother, but if you would like, you are more than welcome to come talk to me anytime, and about anything. I can't tell you what to do but I can listen give you an understanding ear and possibly some guidance or suggestions", he offered kindly. Hannah nodded and he began to walk away. He had just made it a few pews down when Hannah looked up and called out to him. Her turned around and looked at her as if he had known that was going to happen.

"Can I actually take you up on that now?", Hannah asked him as she shifted nervously in her seat. When he nodded and gestured for her to follow along, she stood up and followed behind him to an office a short walk from the doorway that led out to the podium where the priest stood to give his sermons. He took his seat behind his desk as she sat in the one across from him. She was not sure why but she trusted this man, she did not think he would look down on her or judge her no matter what. She wanted to tell him the whole story but did not know where to begin. She stumbled over her words for a moment as the priest waited patiently. 1210 He placed his hands on the desk in from on him.

"I know about Kayla's lifestyle", he said, "It is actually how I met her". Hannah just looked at him and wondered if he had meant what she was thinking. "I spoke to her a few weeks ago and she told me she was moving in with a friend who did the same thing. I'm assuming that you are that friend.", he looked at Hannah as if expecting a response. She nodded her head quickly, feeling as if she were being scolded. He assured her that it was okay and told her that he was not here to judge her. Hannah relaxed in her seat. She began telling the priest about the argument and how it happened, leaving out the gory details of course. She explained the things that had happened leading up to the argument even going weeks back. She sat there talking to the priest for hours, and he listened the entire time with a look of understanding. Hannah had been a little surprised when she had finished and realized that none of it seemed to have shocked him or made him veer from his look of calm understanding. Hannah waited for his response as he sat there for a moment looking deep in though. Finally she broke the silence.

"What are you thinking about?", she asked him.

"I'm wondering what you are wanting to do about it", he said. She thought for a moment.

"Well, I want to make up with Kayla. She has been a good friend to me and I would like to tell her not to move out after all", Hannah said

"Is that going to be enough?", asked the priest. Hannah looked at him confused as she wondered what he had meant by that. "There's a root cause to the problem that I think will still be there even if you make things right with Kayla", he explained. She thought this over for a moment.

"The escorting makes me feel uncomfortable", Hannah finally said, admitting it to herself for the very first time. The priest took a deep breath and nodded.

"But what would I do about my money situation?", she asked him, feeling a little panicked by the idea. He smiled and nodded.

"There are so many options", he said, "and you are young, so all of them are available to you, and if push ever came to shove, you could always come here for help". She thought this over. She realized she did have plenty of options, she could start a business, find work online, keep looking for a job, or maybe even go back to school for an even higher degree. She began to see that she had not exhausted all her options and escorting is not, in fact, her only option. She smiled brightly at this thought. She did not want to be too hasty and quit immediately though. She decided it might be a good idea to wait a couple weeks and make another plan before she completely stopped working as an escort, but just the thought that she would soon be done with it was enough to make her so happy that she almost felt like crying. She thanked him profusely for helping her sort out her thoughts and issues.

"Is there anything else you would like to talk about?", he asked her.

"No", Hannah said, "but if something comes up, I will certainly be back".

"Do you need a ride home? If so, I think I can certainly find you one", he offered.

"Oh, yes thank you so much", she said, grateful that she would not have to walk back with all those bags on her arms. They both stood to leave. As she picked her bags up off the floor, he opened the door and held it for her. On their way out he stopped and spoke to a lady who was cleaning the church. He came back over to Hannah and the lady followed behind him.

"Mrs. Vero is willing to take you home", he said to Hannah gently. Hannah thanked her and the lady said that it was not problem, she was happy to be getting the rest of the day off to spend with her husband who had been extremely ill lately. The priest smiled at Hannah before telling her goodbye for now.

"Goodbye, and thank you", she responded.

Hannah returned home to find that Kayla and all of her things were gone. She tried to call her immediately and got no answer, so she sent an apology in a text message. Ten minutes after she sent the message, Kayla had still not responded, Hannah went to her room to lay down and take a nap. She was completely exhausted from the walk with all the bags of things she had bought, and from the emotional toll her conversation with the priest had taken on her, so she ended up sleeping through the entire night. She woke up to the light shining through the window. The clock by her bed said it was six in the morning. She checked her phone and was disappointed and saddened to see that she had no new messages or missed phone calls. After looking at her schedule she realized she had an appointment with a client later that day. She wanted to cancel the appointment so bad, but with Kayla gone she knew she could not afford to do that if she wanted to keep her apartment. She did not know how she was going to get through the appointment, but she got up and began getting ready, and while she did, she focused on getting into character.

The client she was seeing today had requested a female domination experience which Hannah felt nervous about. She had never been a dom before, so she watched plenty of online porn to gather inspiration, but she was still nervous because she did not see herself as the type of girl who was suited for that kind of thing. She kept the porn in mind as she selected her lingerie for the date. She picked a black bodysuit. It was made from a leather-like material and had straps that went around her thighs. It snapped in the crotch to make her pussy more accessible with the suit on. She took a long shower and shaved before putting the bodysuit on. She loved the plunging neckline that exposed a great deal of cleavage. After blow-drying her hair, she found a pair of stockings and a black pair of stilettos that matched her outfit. Before doing her make-up, she checked her phone in hopes that Kayla had finally texted her back but the only message she had was her client letting her know that he was on the way. Her heart sank even lower, and she tried to put it out of her mind as she put on the finishing touches. She pretended she was applying warpaint instead of makeup, as she took on the tough and unbreakable mentality that she knew she would need to get through the next couple hours. She finally felt ready and even optimistic that this might in fact be beneficial by helping to relieve some of the tension she was feeling. When her phone rang, she answered it and guided the man to her apartment. When she opened the door, a slim dark-skinned guy who looked to be barely in his twenties walked through the door.

Mistress Hannah (FemDom Story)

"Hey there", she said flirtatiously to the guy who stood before her, "so you're the guy who needs some discipline huh?". When he looked at her an expression of excitement and satisfaction came across his face as he nodded his head in eager agreement.

"Yes, I believe I do", he said eagerly.

"To my room, now", she demanded. He followed close behind her and when she pointed in the doorway he went in the room obediently. "What's your name?", Hannah asked him.

"I'm Donny, ma'am", he replied. She began to circle him as if I were a predator ready to strike as she started feeling more in tune with the character she was playing.

"Donny? What kind of fucking name is that? Sissy boy Donny", she teased. He looked down at his feet with embarrassment and whimpered a little. "I am your mistress Donny", she introduced herself before asking, "Do you understand?".

"Yes", he hurriedly replied.

"Yes What?", she demanded.

"Yes, mistress", he quickly corrected.

"You belong to me now Donny", she snapped sternly.

"Yes, mistress", he repeated.

"Do you understand?", she demanded as she walked over and sat on the edge of her bed eyeing him the whole way.

"Yes, mistress", he uttered.

"Now get down on your hands and knees and come here, my Donny. I want to discipline you now.", she declared.

Donny dropped down to the ground onto his hands and knees, quickly crawling over to the edge of the bed where she sat. She gently patted the bed beside her, and he climbed up onto it. "Now kneel over here Donny", she commanded.

As he did as she ordered him to do, she then pulled out a black collar with silver spikes and fastened it tightly around his neck and then clipped on a matching leash. She turned him around to face her and stared deeply into his eyes, with a look of contempt. "You're a bad, bad boy Donny, how should I punish you?", she asked him.

"Severely", he responded with lust in her eyes as he reached up timidly to touch her.

"Don't touch me you dirty slut", she yelled smacking his hand away from her. He pulled back, looking wounded. "Take your pants off", she ordered coyly. He did as he was told as quickly as he could. She took his cock in her hand and squeezed it hard. Her well-manicured nails dug into the soft flesh leaving small red half-moon shapes. He whimpered and she slowly began to stroke his rock-hard dick. She stared up at him with contempt on her face.

"Thank you, mistress", he said gratefully with a wavering voice.

"Do you like that slut?" she sneered.

"Yes, mistress", he admitted with a soft tone.

"You better not cum, not until I give you my permission to", she ordered. He grimaced but told her that he would not. She continued to stroke his cock with her hand and slowly his moans became louder and louder. She could feel his body getting increasingly tense as he struggled to hold back his desire to cum.

"Oh, please mistress", he began to beg. She loved it when they begged. "Please don't make me wait any longer", he choked out.

"I'll tell you when", she smiled. Suddenly, and without any warning, she slapped him hard across the face with the flat part of her hand. He did not even flinch. She continued to do it two more times and then one final time. "Don't you fucking dare cum", she snapped at him, "That was not permission." As he looked at her with tears in his eyes he was filled with shame.

"Yes, mistress" he said again.

"I'll tell you when," she said sternly, as she smiled sweetly.

"Ok, mistress, I understand", he replied.

"Yes, that's what you fucking think", she replied, slapping him again. He could smell her distinctive scent all over the room and his arousal began to grow even more. It was all he could do not to touch her, not to beg her for permission. He did not know how much longer he would be able to hold back the cum. His resolve had begun to break.

"Please don't make me wait any longer", he said in a pleading tone. She just stared at him without a hint of emotion on her face. After a few minutes she slowly began to stroke him faster and faster.

"Alright Donny, my good slut, you may come", she slowly said, deliberately dragging out every word.

"Thank you, mistress", he breathed. He groaned as he came hard into her hand. She felt his tense muscles begin to relax as he finished. She held her hand beneath his nose.

"Well, would you just look at that", she said shoving it close to his face.

"I'm sorry mistress", he cried out.

"Lick it up", she demanded as she looked down at him. He stuck out his tongue and began to lap up the cum on her hand and she began to pet his head. "Good boy, you clean the messes you make", she softly cooed. He nodded at her to let her know he understood. Once he had most of it up, she shoved him backwards onto the bed so that he was looking up at the ceiling.

"Thank you, mistress" he said with tears of shame streaming down his face. She grabbed his face hard in her hands and brought her face close to his. "Now you will please me, my slut", he nodded unable to speak as she threw her leg over him straddling his face. She moved her hips back, pulled her pussy away from his mouth, looked down at him and told him to open his mouth. He did as he had been instructed and she spat directly into his mouth.

"Thank you, mistress", he said with a smile of gratitude as she buried his face back into her pussy and began to rock her hips back and forth. He stuck his tongue out and she moaned at the feeling of his hot wet tongue on her wet pussy. She grabbed a handful of his hair and used it to pull his face harder against her pussy and she positioned herself on top of his face so that he could not breathe. She used the leash to pull him even harder against her. She remained there for a moment. When she pulled away and gave him access to air he gasped for breath as she began riding his face again. He looked up at her appreciatively. "You like that don't you?", she asked with a smile. He nodded his head at her as he held his tongue out continuing to taste her sweet pussy.

"I love it, my mistress", he confirmed. She looked down at him with disdain and rode his face harder, using his face for her own pleasure. She began to moan a little as he flicked his tongue against her clit.

"Mmmm, yes my slut. That feels so good", she said. He moaned at the affirmation he had given her, and he began to flick his tongue against her clit even faster.

Suddenly she felt pleasure and warmth overcome her as she began to come hard against his face. He moaned loudly and began to cry out in pleasure at the taste of her come. When she was done, she ordered for him to stop. "You did good slut", she said as she looked at him approvingly. "Have you ever been owned by a mistress before?", she asked.

"No, mistress", he responded shyly. She thought this over for a moment before instructing him to get back on the floor and on his knees. She did as he was told without a word. She looked down at him and raised her foot up to his eye level, dangling it in front od his face as if it were a prize. He reached out to touch it, but she snatched it away with a laugh. She pressed a toe against his lips as he kept his hands down at his side. He opened his mouth and let her toes slide in. She noticed his eyes were shut tight.

"Look at me slut", she said calmly. He opened his eyes wide and looked at his mistress feeling his hot desire rushing back to him. She saw his cock begin to grow and become hard once again and laughed at the sight. With her foot still in his mouth she began to speak. "Do you understand what being my sub means?", she asked. She removed her foot and placed it back onto the floor. As she did he looked at it as if he were a dog and she was taking his treat.

"I think so mistress", he said. She went on to explain to him that she would cause him pain, but that in turn would give him pleasure.

"Do you love me, slut?", she questioned.

116

"Yes, mistress", he answered. She picked up a riding crop from her dresser and smacked him hard with it on his thigh. "No slut", she said, "You do not love me, in fact slut you do not know me", she sternly stated as she hit his thigh again with the crop. He winced a little at the sting and he agreed.

"I understand mistress, I do not love you", he said.

"Good slut", she said patting his head affectionately. "Now, who do you belong to bitch", she asked as she rested her heel on his thigh and began to press her weight down as the heel sank into his thigh.

"You do my mistress, I am your worthless slut", he said looking at her as the pain became apparent on her face. His cock was now fully erect.

"Do you want to stick that filthy thing in me, slut?", she asked him as she gestured to his dick.

"I would love to slut, but only if it pleases you", he responded with a hopeful look.

"That will never please me, you disgusting slut", she scoffed. He looked away from her and she dug her heel even deeper. "Don't look away from me", she demanded. He snapped his eyes back and locked his gaze with hers.

"Mistress?", he said cautiously.

"What do you want, slut?", she asked.

"May I please stroke my cock?", he asked her.

"Yes, I'll allow it", she said. She watched as he gripped his cock and started pumping his hand up and down the shaft. "Faster slut, but do not come without asking", she reminded.

"Yes, mistress", he said as he began to pick up the pace.

"Does it feel good?", she asked him. He nodded and she saw his muscles begin to twitch. She had no intention on letting him come that fast. She demanded him to stop, and he obediently took his hand away from his cock. She began to slowly rub her foot across his cock, and he whimpered as he tried to hold back his urge to come. She gazed down at him unenthusiastically as she continued stroking him with her foot. "You can come now slut", she chimed. And she immediately did. It spurted out all over her foot. She looked at him with disgust.

"Now clean it up", she commanded. He immediately did as he was told. Once her foot was clean, she put it back into her shoe. "You've been a good slut today", she said with a smile. "Now it is time for you to leave. Mistress is tired now", she said. He began to object but she cut him off before he could get it out. "You will do as you're told", she screamed. He whimpered and got up. He gathered his clothes and put them on. When he was done, he shyly sat an envelope on the table beside her bed. He kept his head down like a wounded animal as he left, not saying another word to his new mistress.

She breathed a heavy sigh of relief once he left. She was surprised to find that this was one of the rare occasions that she did not feel uneasy after a date. She glanced at her phone and saw a text from Daryl. He was the only other client that she did not feel uncomfortable with. He requested to see both Hannah and the friend she had told him about. He explained that he had bought a game that required at least three players, and he wanted to play it. He clarified that it was a sex game that he had picked up at the porn store. Hannah felt hopeful that this might be her ticket to get Kayla to talk to her again. He offered them each five hundred and Hannah told him that she would see if she could make it happen. She immediately texted Kayla about it but did not hear anything back. Hannah fell asleep waiting for a response from Kayla. Hannah woke up to a loud bang on the door. She rolled out of bed and groggily made her way to the door and opened it. When she saw Kayla standing there her eyes went wide.

"Sorry for waking you up, I had to come by to let you know that I want to do that date. I broke my phone, and I can read your messages, but I can't respond. I get my replacement tomorrow", Kayla explained.

"I'm really sorry", Hannah began. Kayla flicked her wrist in a gesture that meant it's no big deal. When Hannah asked her to come back, Kayla looked at her with an unsure expression.

"Let's just see how things go, okay?", Kayla said. Hannah felt terrible about her being back at the hotel, but she understood Kayla's apprehensiveness. The two girls sat and talked for a bit and Hannah messaged Daryl and set the appointment for a few days out. Hannah told Kayla all about her talk with the priest and how she figured out that escorting was not right for her.

"He even told me that if it came down to it, I could come to him for help", Hannah said.

"Watch out, he might be trying to turn you into a nun", Kayla joked. Hannah told her that she had been considering her options.

"I could probably find work if I tried a little harder", she said, "but, I don't know, it might be easier to just find a wealthy guy who is not too bad on the eyes and get him to marry me". She told Kayla that she had also considered going back to school but said she doubted she would. She felt done with that part of her life and wanted to move on from it. Kayla suggested that Hannah also consider doing webcam modeling or something like that, but Hannah doubted she would be able to do that. She could hardly manage to keep up with her Facebook account. Keeping up with getting on the webcam every day seemed like an impossible task for her. They discussed a few ideas Hannah had for businesses she had considered starting up as well, but she was not sure how she would be able to get the money she needed for stat-up costs.

"I just know I can not do much more of this escorting thing. I'm just not cut out for it", Hannah finished.

"I guess it's to the cloister with ya then", Kayla said laughing.

"I do love to go from one extreme to the next", Hannah admitted. Kayla stood to leave, and Hannah began to object.

"I've really got to run a few errands", Kayla insisted. Hannah hugged her tight and gave her one last apology before letting Kayla walk away.

"I'll see you in a few days for the appointment with Daryl?", she asked.

"Of course, I'll be here right at three", Kayla promised. Hannah closed and locked the door behind Kayla when she left and sat of the couch. She kept going through the options in her head. She considered the possibility of dating one of her clients. She thought through them and it seemed to her that many of them liked her enough that they would probably be happy to date her. She thought a few of them would probably even agree to marry her out the gate, but she did not know for sure if that would be much better than her current situation. She made herself a drink and went to her room, vowing to put it out of her mind for the night. After taking a moment to appreciate the fact that Kayla, did not hate her as she had been beginning to think, she grabbed the remote and switched the television on and began flipping through some channels. She finally settled on a lifetime movie, which she quickly fell asleep to.

The next few days Kayla spent considering and continuing to research all of her available options. She even stumbled across some loans and grants for business start-ups, that she felt she had a fairly good chance of being able to get. She got lonely and texted Kayla a few times, but she seemed to be staying busy most of the time, all-of-a-sudden. Which made Hannah question whether she might actually be somewhat angry at her. She decided that she would discuss it with Hannah either before or after their upcoming date with Daryl. Hannah was actually beginning to look forward to that date, sitting around the apartment by herself was no fun at all, especially after being so used to having Kayla around all the time.

The day of the appointment finally came. Kayla had her new phone finally working right so Hannah was able to send her a message to ask when she would be coming. Around ten in the morning Kayla responded saying that she was on her way and that she was going to come early so they could get ready together. When she read the text, Hannah squealed with excitement. She missed her friend and was ready to spend some time with her and try to get things back to normal between them. Hannah jumped in the shower before Kayla arrived so that she would not have to take the time to do it while she was there. Then she went ahead and pre-made a couple of drinks for them to sip on before Daryl arrived. She texted him to confirm the time and he responded saying that he would be there. Hannah left the door unlocked as she blow-dried her hair so that if she did not hear the knock, Kayla could just walk in. As Hannah expected she would she did walk in. So, when she came out the bathroom, Kayla accidentally startled Hannah. They drank and got caught up on all the recent happenings. Hannah did a lot more listening than talking because her last few days had been spent at home not doing much at all. Kayla told Hannah about how the woman who had brought her home from the church that day, Mrs. Vero, had unfortunately lost her husband to cancer. Hannah felt terrible and decided to send flowers to the upcoming funeral.

Game Night (Sex Game Story)

It was getting close to time for Daryl to arrive so both Hannah and Kayla got on some lingerie and took care of all the last-minute details they needed to do before he arrived. The knock on the door came a little earlier than expected and Kayla had to answer the door and keep Daryl busy for a moment so Hannah could finish getting ready. When she joined them in the living room Daryl was excitedly showing Kayla the game that he was wanting them to play with him and Kayla was listening intently as he explained it.

"Hey guys, what's up?", Kayla asked as she walked into the room.

"Just checking out this game that Daryl brought for us to play", Kayla responded.

"What's the game called?", Hannah asked as looked down at the cards on the table.

"Dirty Deeds", Daryl said with an unmistakable excitement in his voice. Hannah offered Daryl a drink, and he said he could have just one, so she quickly made three mixed drinks and they sat in a circle around the coffee table as Daryl shuffled the cards.

"The player to the left of the dealer goes first so Kayla it's your go", Daryl said once he got the cards shuffled. Kayla picked a card from the stack and read it.

"Who do I do it to?", Kayla asked.

"It's your choice", Daryl responded. Kayla began reading her card aloud.

"Wait so how do we declare a winner?", Kayla asked.

"How about whoever gets Daryl's come wins?", Hannah suggested with a mischievous grin.

"Okay", Kayla said, feeling confident that she could make Daryl come faster than Hannah could.

"Alright", said Daryl, "But I get to pick one of your cards for you ladies to work on each other.

"Kiss your lover from head to toe for five minutes", she said. Then she made a thinking face and smiled over at Daryl. His cheeks tuned slightly red as she kissed the top of his head. She made a trail of kisses down to the collar of his shirt. She began unbuttoning the shirt leaving a kiss where each button had been. She unbuttoned his pants and kissed her way down his cock as she pulled off his pants and boxers. She kissed all the way down his legs and the tops of his feet. She left one final kiss on the tip of his pinky toe and then smiled up at him. They all three laughed and then Kayla turned to Hannah.

"It's your turn", she said to Hannah smiling. Hannah selected a card from the top of the pile and turned it over and read it to herself.

"I have to give one of you oral for twenty-five minutes", Hannah said smiling. Daryl quickly pointed to Kayla and Hannah smiled at him. "Does that mean you are using what might be your one chance to see some girl-on-girl action?", she asked him teasingly.

"Yes I am. This one is for you and Kayla", Daryl declared with a playful smile as he decided to use his ability to make one of the girls chose the other.

"Kayla get those panties out of my way", Hannah said winking at Daryl playfully. She got down onto her knees in the floor between Kayla's legs and began softly began kissing up her thigh as she slowly made her way over to her clit, then she began flicking it with her tongue. Hannah lightly nibbled at her clit before she plunged her tongue into Kayla's tight hole. She enjoyed the taste of Kayla's arousal on her tongue. Hannah really began to get into it as she vivaciously licked all over Kayla's wet pussy. She knew she only had twenty-five minutes and she wanted to make Kayla come. Kayla began to squirm and move her hips pushing herself eagerly against Hannah's warm wet tongue. She threw her head back and then moaned loudly as Hannah sucked gently on her clit.

"Oh fuck, yes, lick my pussy," Kayla said, holding her hand on the top of Hannah's head. Hannah briefly looked up and saw Daryl standing there watching her longingly as he rubbed his cock at the sight of them. The twenty-five minutes were nearly up so Hannah picked up her pace. She licked and sucked at Kayla's swollen wet pussy with everything she had. When Kayla's legs began to shake and tremble, she flicked her tongue against faster against Kayla's clit knowing that she was getting close to her climax. Warm sweet liquid suddenly began gushing out of Kayla's pussy just in time. When she finished coming, there was quite a mess left behind. Hannah had just enough time remaining to lick up her sweet juices as she moaned and trembled. Then Kayla's body went limp as she relaxed her muscles, and she began to pant, and she tried to catch her breathe. Hannah looked up at Kayla with a proud expression.

"Do I get Bonus points for that?", she asked jokingly. Daryl and Kayla both busted out laughing at Hannah's question. As Hannah wiped her mouth clean and took a sip from her drink. Hannah then had to quickly run to the restroom so that she could pee because the alcohol was filling her bladder quickly.

"You should! Oh my, that was good", Kayla breathed. "You've been holding out on me bitch", she half joked as she struggled to regain her composure. They all three laughed in unison as they returned to their seats around the coffee table to resume the game. Daryl rubbed his hands together for luck before picking up a card up. He took a sip of his drink and then looked at his card. Both girls looked at him expectantly as he immediately read the card aloud.

"Tease one player's nipples for five minutes.", he said shrugging clearly unimpressed by the card he had drawn. He looked over at Kayla who was still trying to catch her breathe from the intense orgasm she had just experienced, "I'll give you a rest my dear", he said kindly before making his way over to where Hannah was sitting looking as if she were getting bored. "You look like you could use some excitement", he said to Hannah who quickly nodded her head and smiled in response. He pulled the bralette of her lingerie set out of his way and began to circle her nipples lightly with the tip of his tongue. He made each circle smaller and smaller until the tip of his tongue touched the very tip of her perky little nipples. Hannah moaned, feeling her pussy tingle with excitement as if it were linked to her nipples. She moaned as he nibbled and sucked on her hard ready nipples. Kayla touched Daryl's cock and she noticed that it was fully erect and harder than she had ever felt it. She could not help but stroke it a few times as he teased Hannah's nipples. He could feel how badly she wanted to be fucked by him and he wanted to fuck her just as badly. He wanted to touch and play with that hot wet pussy and he was having a tough time struggling to resist the urge. Suddenly, the timer went off loudly reminding them that their time was up, and Hannah looked at him and bit her lip seductively. Daryl had trouble pulling himself away, but he did regardless. It was now Kayla's turn again, so she grabbed a card from the deck. She looked at the card with confusion and then she lowered it so everyone could see why she looked so confused.

"It just has a pair of handcuffs on it, with no words", she said unsure of what that meant. Daryl remembered that he had forgotten to explain this part of the game, and he pulled his bag close to him and he took out eight items that were typically used for sexual purposes and laid them all out in front of them. He explained that she did not have to take a turn now, and that getting that card meant that the next task that she was to select, had to be done with the handcuffs somehow being used. Daryl picked up the pair of handcuffs. They were lined with black fur to make them more comfortable for the person wearing them. He sat them on the table close to Kayla so that she had them in her reach when it came time to use them. Hannah picked up a card slowly to build suspense. She peeked at it for a moment and made eye contact with both Kayla, and then Daryl before beginning to read it aloud.

"Give one player a five-minute lap dance", she read with a smile. Hannah turned up the volume on the music and began to seductively grind her mostly nude body against Daryl. She felt his hard cock rubbing against her ass as she danced. The feeling of it made her pussy get very wet. He could feel the wetness when he ran his hand across her pussy. She turned to face him, and he felt her breath against his ear as she lightly nibbled it. As she moved her body with the music, he explored every inch of her skin with his hands. He stared at the way her body moved as if he were in a trance. He wanted to do terrible things to her. He imagined himself licking her, touching her, and fucking her. The timer went off and to Daryl's dismay, she was done He clapped his hands together a few times slowly to show his appreciation. Hannah loved the impressed look on his face. Daryl did not say a word before he selected a card from the pile on the table.

"Spank a player for five minutes", Daryl read as if he were still deciding. "Kayla, you really have been being such a bad girl tonight", he said as he gestured for Kayla to come over to him. She crawled over to him without any objections and obediently bent herself over his knee as she braced herself for the first blow. Daryl pulled her panties down to her knees, exposing her bare ass cheeks, which were begging to be spanked. He smacked her hard on her ass and she moaned a response. He began slapping her plump bottom repeatedly, using more strength with each blow. After a minute Kayla winced with every smack as she felt his hand beginning to sting against her ass, badly. After two minutes Daryl noticed her ass was getting red and welted. This only made him want to smack her harder. Three minutes in her ass was hot to the touch, and she was groaning with a mix of pleasure and fiery pain. At four minutes in she was on fire and tears began coming from her eyes. Kayla whimpered through the last few blows Daryl delivered. When he was done, he complemented Kayla on withstanding that pain. Kayla did not mind; she had loved every second of it. She was feeling a bit overstimulated, so she called for a much-needed break so using the excuse that she was thirsty and needed to get them some fresh drinks. Daryl refused to drink any more alcohol because he had to drive home, so Kayla came back with just two mixed drinks and a bottle of water, which Daryl graciously accepted. She cautiously picked a card up and read it out loud to the group.

"Fuck one player for twenty fine minutes", she said looking around as if she did not know who she should pick. "So, I have to use the handcuffs during this, right?", she clarified.

"That's right", Daryl said nodding. Kayla asked Daryl to lay down, flat on his back. He smiled with a knowing expression and did as he was instructed to do. "I'm not going to make this easy for you", he promised with a devilish smile.

"Nor will I make it easy for you", she said with a calm confidence as she straddled his cock, running her pussy against it seductively where it was resting between her long tan legs. She grabbed his hands and raised them above his head forcefully. He gazed at her as if challenging her to give it her all. She used the handcuffs to lock his hands securely around the leg of the coffee table so that he could not touch her. Then she took hold of his cock with both of her hands and began to slide the thick cock straight into her tight wet pussy. He moaned in satisfaction as he felt his member being squeezed hard by her pussy. He liked the helpless feeling he got from being cuffed and she embraced the feeling of control that came from Daryl being restrained and unable to do anything to stop her, not that he wanted to. She rocked her hips back and forth slowly easing his cock deeper and deeper inside of her tiny hole.

"Oh Yeah, that feels so fucking good", Daryl said with a growl as he admired her perky beautiful tits. He loved how they bounced vigorously up and down with the force of her fucking him. Each time she sped up and began to fuck him harder they began bouncing with even more force than before. He had almost forgotten that Hannah was in the room. He glanced over at Hannah who was sitting on the couch watching them intently and reminded himself to resist any urges to come. He knew the urge would probably begin to surface soon, so he braced himself for it and tried to prepare so that he would not let himself come in Kayla's ready pussy. This cum belongs to Hannah, he said trying to convince his body to hold back. As Kayla bounced up and down on his cock, he felt his orgasm building despite his attempts to stifle it. Suddenly, the timer began to ding, and Daryl breathed a sigh of relief at having been able to hold himself back from his orgasm. Kayla looked slightly disappointed by this, and Daryl writhed with sexual frustration, because of the fact that he had gotten so close, but did not get to come, but he know it would soon happen. He found solace in the knowledge that he would probably have another opportunity very soon, so he convinced himself that he was not too worried about it. Kayla slowly opened the locks of the handcuffs to release Daryl. Everyone settled back around the coffee table without talking much. Both ladies were plotting attempting to devise a plan that would assist them in winning this game. As they contemplated strategies, Hannah felt hopeful as she picked up her next card and read it. First to herself, then to everyone else. She flipped her card over with a disappointed expression. On the card there was a vibrator. Which meant she did not get a turn this round. Daryl looked at her apologetically as he flipped the next card.

"Make out with any player for five minutes", he scowled a little and rolled his eyes at the card. Daryl pointed over to Hannah to let her know that he had selected her. He was disappointed by his card. He figured that there was no way Hannah could make him come by making out with him. They began passionately kissing, and the timer was dinging before they knew it. Kayla selected a card and revealed that it had a paddle on it. Her shoulders slumped a little as she realized she was not getting a turn this round.

"Damn, I so thought I had this", Kayla said with a disappointed tone, "You really didn't make it easy on me did you Daryl?", she said. Hannah eagerly picked her next card up. She smiled when she saw what it said.

"Sixty-nine with another player for ten minutes", She read with a triumphant smile. She had already made Daryl come many times before with her mouth, and she knew exactly what she had to do and how he liked his cock licked, but ten minutes is not much time at all, so she knew that she had to be on her best game and perform fast to get it done before the timer began to. Hannah pointed at Daryl and seductively motioned for him to come to her. He laid down on the floor flat on his back and took in the view as Hannah positioned herself on top of him. His cock was still hard from the last round, and he felt ready to come at any moment.

"I love all this attention I'm getting, Thanks so much, ladies", he said smiling at both girls. "Thank you both for playing this game with me, and with so much enthusiasm. You girls are amazing.", he said affectionately and as if the game had already ended. Both girls agreed that they were having a great time with this adventurous little card game, and they had both gotten to be competitive with it. Hannah crawled on top of Daryl and took his entire cock into her mouth as she straddled his face. He tasted her sweet pussy and moaned. She bobbed her head up and down on his cock, pushing it far back into her throat.

"Mmmm baby, you are delicious", he said to Hannah appreciatively. She felt his cock twinge in her mouth, and she knew he would soon be coming.

"Thank you", she said smiling up at Daryl with appreciation. "I love sucking your fat cock", she enthusiastically stated before plunging his cock into the back of her throat. She circled the tip of his head with her tongue, and he moaned and arched his back as he felt the come building up inside of him. She sucked on it hard as she ran her tongue up and down the entire length of his cock. He buried his face into her pussy and moaned loudly into it. She heard his moans become louder and she looked up at the expression of pure ecstasy on his face. He looked back down at her and he suddenly felt himself beginning to erupt inside of her mouth. It came out hard and fast and she hungrily swallowed it in full gulps as it did. When she knew she had sucked his cock completely dry, she saved the last little bit of his come in her mouth and stuck her tongue out to show Kayla that she had won the game. Daryl said goodbye to each of the girls, hugged them each tightly, and thanked them both for a wonderful time.

"I hope I get to see you again", Kayla flirted as she pushed a strand of hair out of her face.

"I definitely think you will", Daryl responded with a wink in her direction.

"That was actually really fun", Hannah exclaimed after Daryl had left and she had closed the door. She turned to look at Kayla excitedly thinking that they could maybe hang out for the night.

"I had a blast", Kayla agreed. "But now I'm tired, and I really need to get to bed", Kayla said yawning. She began to gather her things to get ready to leave. Hannah wanted to protest, but she decided it would be best not to do that, despite the pit she felt deep in her stomach. They said their goodbyes and hugged one another, and when Kayla left, Hannah looked around her big empty apartment feeling lonely. She had a lot of fun tonight with Kayla and Daryl. She did not have those awful feelings that typically followed Hannah's dates, but regardless; she knew that this was a rare exception, and she could not bear to continue doing this to herself. She felt stuck and bound by her financial needs. She remained unsure of what to do to escape this life that had begun to wear her down. She got out her laptop and began doing research again to try to find a solution. After searching the web for various options for a couple of hours she somehow ended up on the catholic church's website. She knew Kayla had just been kidding when she suggested that Hannah become a nun, but she was curious about it. The church had an admirable set of values, and to her it seemed it might be one her quickest, easiest and safest option out of this deplorable life she had found herself living. She knew she desired a life with strong values and morals, and to her this option seemed like it was perfectly aligned with what she wanted out of life. She was also afraid that she would fall back into escorting if ever she started to struggle with money, and being a nun seemed like a solid way of mitigating that risk.

She fell asleep in front of her computer with a web page on the typical processes of becoming a nun pulled up in front of her. She snapped awake still at her computer. She got up and threw on some of the most modest clothes she had and made her way down to the church on foot. When she got there, she walked inside the building and she was overcome with a homey feeling that made her feel as though she belonged there. She immediately saw the priest at the front of the room, hovering over some papers at his podium and she walked directly up to him.

"Oh, what a nice surprise", he said smiling at Hannah with a bright smile.

"Hey father, can I please have a word with you in private?", she asked him quietly.

"Of course,", he responded kindly. He immediately put down the papers that he had been working on filling out and he led Hannah back to his office where they had spoken for the first time not so long ago. Once there they both sat down in the exact spots they had been in for their last conversation, facing each other. Hannah took on a thoughtful expression, and the priest patiently waited as she gathered her words and tried to carefully chose them.

"What is the process of becoming a nun?", she plainly asked, unsure of how to more tactfully ease into the conversation. The priest looked at her lovingly as he thought about her question and considered how to best answer it.

"That's a huge commitment", he began, "but if you are really serious, I would be honored to help you get there". They sat and spoke about it for a while. He gave her a brief rundown of the steps involved in becoming a nun. He told her that technically, she was too young to join the nuns, but then he told her that with his recommendation, they would likely make an exception for her. Hannah was thrilled to hear this. He just said that she needed to prove to him that she really was committed to it. She began trying to convince the priest that she was completely committed immediately. She began to spend most of her free time volunteering at the church and she even began learning the scripture from the bible. At her core she still did not honestly have the unwavering faith and belief that most of the church goers seemed to possess, but she loved the values and character of the church and that is what drove her to take this path. She was excited about the prospect of doing services for her community and helping others. She had always felt great anytime she was doing something kind for someone else. The other thing that drover her was the idea of being free of the worries of money and sex and the many other things that were considered a sin. She was at the church volunteering, working with the children in the community one day when Kayla happened to stop by the church and had spotted her. She called out to Hannah to get her attention but Hannah could not hear her over all the kids yelling excitedly.

"What is she doing here?", she asked herself. She finally got Hannah's attention. "Hey, what are you doing?", she asked as she approached Hannah.

"I'm just helping out", Hannah replied.

"I thought you did not like it here", Kayla inquired.

"I didn't say I didn't like it. I just felt out of place. Lately I have begun to feel more like I belong", she explained. Kayla nodded in agreement. Hannah did not mention to Kayla that she was trying to join the nuns.

"Do you want to hang out later?", Kayla asked Hannah nonchalantly.

"Sure", Kayla responded, "I will be done here in about an hour then I was planning to head back home". Kayla looked at her with a curious expression for a moment before turning to walk away. A few hours later she texted Hannah to see if she had made it back home. Kayla had some news to give Hannah that she thought she would be thrilled to hear. When Hannah responded saying that she was in fact home, Kayla headed straight over to her apartment. On the way there she pondered reasons why Hannah would have suddenly become interested in the church.

"Hey", Hannah said to Kayla as she opened the door.

"Hey", Kayla responded. "Are you okay?", Kayla asked with concern apparent on her face.

"Of course, why? What is up?", Hannah inquired.

"I'm just wondering about your sudden interest in the church", Kayla said quizzically as she probed for answers.

"It's just that the church has a lot of resources that could help me out of my current situation. You know how much I cannot stand escorting and I like the values they carry at the church", Hannah added. Kayla nodded slowly.

"Anyway, I noticed you took your ad down", Kayla said.

"Yeah, I'm only seeing my regulars now", Hannah said without stating any reasons.

"I have a client who has been interested in seeing you for a while. I showed him a picture of you and ever since he keeps asking about you every time, I see him", Kayla mentioned. "Should I send him your way or are you not taking on any new clients at all?", Kayla asked. Hannah thought it over.

"I don't mind seeing him", Hannah said trying to hide her reluctance. She knew she needed the money badly, so she agreed despite her feeling of repulsion by the notion. She was already getting behind on rent again after just getting completely caught up.

"Also, I would consider moving back in if you wanted", Kayla suggested. Hannah agreed excitedly asnd told Kayla that she could do so immediately.

"It's been really lonely around here since you left", she explained. Kayla went back to her hotel and got her stuff and Hannah stayed this time, remembering how scared she had been the last time she went. Kayla quickly moved back into the apartment the following day after making Hannah promise that she would not try to kick Kayla out again without giving her adequate notice. Kayla went ahead and paid her half of the month since she knew that Hannah was behind and struggling to get caught up on all of the bills by herself. Kayla set the date with her client up a few days out for Hannah. Hannah was glad she had because she had not been working much lately, so she felt that she needed the time to prepare for the date mentally. Those few days went by incredibly fast especially since she now had Kayla around again. Hannah liked the relief from the loneliness that Kayla provided. They were back to spending most of their free time hanging out, and drinking and watching movies, which was not very much since Hannah has so many commitments to the church now. On the day of the date, Hannah was relaxing in her room after just waking up when she suddenly heard Kayla banging hard on her bedroom door.

Daddy's Little Girl (BDSM)

"What?", Hannah called wondering why Kayla felt the need to pound on her door so early in the morning. She felt frustrated by it but tried to hold it back so that she did not get snappy or mean with Kayla. She took a few calming breaths and waited for Kayla to respond.

"Did you forget about the client coming?", Kayla urgently called through the door. Hannah looked at the time and began to panic.

"Oh, shit", she grumbled. Then she called out to Kayla that she was getting ready as fast as she could. She asked Kayla to send the client a text to ask him to push the appointment back an hour or so. Luckily, the client was fine with pushing back the appointment by a half hour. This gave Hannah just enough time to get herself ready. She quickly ran across the hall and got straight in the shower. She rushed through the entire process of shaving, washing, doing her hair and make-up, and getting herself dressed, but at the end she was satisfied with the outcome as she looked at herself in the mirror. She picked a cute body harness that she had recently bought to wear since she knew that this client was interested in BDSM. Hannah knew she was good at being a sub, and she was much more comfortable with that than she was with being a dom, so she definitely felt more comfortable with this date. She finished getting

141

ready just in time and ran to the door to let the client inside. Kayla left to run some errands so her and this new client had the apartment to themselves. He came inside with a duffle bag over his shoulder and did not say a word when Hannah greeted him. She quickly became nervous due to his silent and tough demeanor and began to ramble on about senseless things.

"Silence!", he ordered loudly having apparently had enough of her talking. Hannah abruptly stopped talking and watched him with a shocked, wide-eyed expression as he dropped his bag to the floor with a thud. He pulled out a ball gag and walked over to Hannah holding it out. When he put it up to her mouth, she opened wide and let him fasten it around her head. He walked back to his bag and pulled some restraints our of it. He made his way back over to Hannah and fastened thick leather straps to each of her wrists, and then to each of her ankles. He clipped the wrist straps to the back of her body harness so that her hands were secured tightly behind her back. He looked at her directly in her eyes. "When you address me, you will call me daddy, do you understand?", he said sternly as he looked her in the eyes. He removed the gag from her mouth long enough for her to answer him.

"Yes daddy", she said sweetly. Her pussy got wet just from saying those words to this strange man. He replaced the ball gag then walked back over to his bag. He came back with a paddle in one hand, and his fist closed around something else. He saw Hannah looking at his hand curiously, so he held his hand out in front of her. When he unclenched his fist, Hannah saw two nipple clamps in his hand. One at a time, he fastened them both to her nipples. Then he yanked the first one off. Hannah yelped at the pain, and the man smiled sadistically at Hannah. He clamped it back onto her nipple before bending her over his knee and smacking her hard on the ass with the wooden paddle a few times. She whimpered and her ass felt as if it had been set on fire as he delivered each blow with all his might. Suddenly he was grabbing her hair and forcing her to her knees. He held onto her hair as he unbuttoned his pants and took out his cock. Then he shoved his long hard cock deep into Hannah's throat so that she gagged on it. He used her hair to fuck her in the mouth. She gagged so hard tears began streaking down her cheeks leaving a trail of black eyeliner and mascara all the way down. When he was satisfied, he pulled her to her feet. He went back to his bag and pulled something rather large from it. It was a board, and it had clips on it to fasten her restraints to. He pulled Hannah over to the board and began attaching her restraints in various places. When he was happy with the position she was in, he slid his cock into her groaning as he entered her dripping wet pussy. For a moment he fucked her hard. Without any warning he reached up and yanked one of the nipples clamps off.

"Ouch", she cried out in pain. She winced as she felt her nipple becoming harder from the pain of the clamp being ripped carelessly from her soft tiny nipple. A tear rand down her cheek and he wiped it off with his hand.

"Calm down slut," he responded. "This is just a little reminder of who's in control. Don't forget to call me daddy." He thrust his cock in and out of her pussy, as he did, he pulled the nipple other clamp off her. She

143

screamed in pain, and he vigorously slammed his cock into her pussy over and over. He pulled his cock out and unclipped the restraints so he could flip Hannah onto her back. "I want you to come now", he said as he lowered his face down into her eager pussy.

"Yes daddy", she responded. He began to lick her pussy. He flicked his tongue back and forth across her clit as she moaned. He ate her pussy so good she came within minutes. She squirted hot come from her pussy. He kept licking her and she continued to come for several minutes. When she was done, he flipped her onto her hands and knees and fastened her into position on the board. He resumed slamming his cock into her now soaked pussy. He began to pant harder and harder, and his moans got increasingly loud. Her tight pussy made his cock begin to spasm and not long after that he reached his orgasm despite his attempts to hold it back. He filled her pussy with his hot cum. He leaned over her and took the time to catch his breath. He did not want to be done. He decided he was not done.

"Lick it clean", he ordered as he positioned his cock directly in front of her face. She opened her mouth and he thrusted himself inside. She began sucking his cock again and did so eagerly. Her hands reached up and she began rubbing her swollen clit. It was only a minute before she screamed out in pure ecstasy. She arched her back as waves of orgasmic pleasure gripped her body. She continued moaning loudly and her body continued to spasm in what seemed like wave after wave of pleasure, almost too much to handle. He pulled out of her soaked pussy and stood up. He sat on the board and reached around her, grabbing her arms and pulling her down until her shoulders rested on the board. She was completely exposed, and at his mercy. He positioned his cock at the entrance to her pussy and began to slowly slide it into her soaking wet, dripping cunt. She was completely wet and ready for him to fuck her. She screamed out and again begged him to fuck her harder. He pushed even deeper inside her. She was almost aching to be filled by his cock. He continued sliding his cock into her slowly. She clenched her eyes closed, only vaguely aware of the waves of pleasure that were starting to overwhelm her body. He could feel her pussy walls begin to clamp down on his cock, wanting his cock to fill them to the brim. He moved his hands up her arms and wrapped them around her neck. He placed his hands on her shoulders and began pushing even harder into her pussy. She begged him to fuck her harder. She could feel him lift on his toes and was pretty sure he could feel her wet, tight pussy engulfing his cock. He began to slam his cock deeper and deeper into her pussy.

"Oh God yes", she screamed. He began to gasp, and this body jerked involuntarily as he felt his orgasm getting close. He grabbed her tits and squeezed them hard. She squealed in pain and pleasure as he pulled her tits back and forth as he continued to fuck her. It seemed like he had fucked her harder and longer than she had ever been fucked before, and she could not believe he was still going. As the last wave of orgasmic pleasure washed over her, he started to come so hard within her that it almost felt as if he had been fucking her nonstop for hours.

"That's it daddy, fuck your baby girl's pussy. Fuck her pussy! I can feel it!" she cried out with delight. He could feel himself pumping his thick cum into her as he tried to thrust every last drop into her tiny pussy. He could feel her pussy grabbing at his cock and taking it inside of her again. He felt the last flood of his cum fill her up as if he had exploded in her pussy. She screamed out in pleasure. Then they both collapsed on the board, panting hard as the room spun around them.

"That's my good girl", he whispered in her ear as he softly petted her head and continued to lay there trying to catch his breathe. She whimpered beneath him feeling utterly exhausted as the shame of what she had just done began to take hold. She silently wished he would leave, but he took his time. He finished catching his breath, and then went straight to the bathroom to clean himself up without saying a word to her or acknowledging her in any way. Then he slowly and methodically packed all of his things into the duffel bag he had arrived with. He lightly kissed her forehead before he walked out of the apartment door. Hannah quickly jumped up and locked the door behind him. She went to her room and began to cry into her pillow until she fell into a deep sleep. Her eyes were swollen and puffy from crying when she woke up. She realized she was nearly late for an important event at the church that the priest had asked her to attend.

"Shit", she cussed under her breathe as she got up and jumped in the shower. Every step she took was a painful reminder of what had happened before she went to sleep thanks to her sore and swollen pussy. She tried to ignore it as she finished getting herself ready. She heard Kayla come in the door and so Hannah asked her for a ride down to the church. Kayla said she would take her, and Hannah thanked her. Hannah quickly finished getting ready and then the girls got into the car. Kayla decided to stay at the church for the event, which neither of them were sure exactly what the purpose for it was. The pews were filled with people as the priest walked to the front of the room. He began speaking about celebrating life and having gratitude for our blessings. Hannah periodically nodded her head in agreement. She almost did not hear it when he called out her name. He was looking at her expectantly and so was half the people in the room. He gestured for her to come up to the stage, so she slowly stood. Suddenly she realized what he had said before her name. Sister, he had said Sister Hannah. Her mouth fell open as the realization struck her. That meant she finally had been accepted into the ranks of the nuns. She looked back at Kayla's shocked and confused expression, but she could not help but beam with pride at the news. She blushed when she realized the room was clapping loudly for her. Not long after, as she stood in a group of her new sisters, as people began to file out of the room. She approached the priest to ask if she could go speak to Kayla for a moment. He nodded an affirmation and so she ran down the aisle to where her friend stood waiting.

"I was kidding when I suggested you become a nun, but you actually did it", she blurted out in a mix of tears and laughter. Hannah shrugged and began to explain that she had wanted so bad to be free of the worries that had

147

begun plaguing her since she had left college and became an escort. She expressed her desire to do good for the world and told Kayla that she felt that this life had been calling out to her for some time now. The shock did not leave Kayla's face, but she nodded realizing that she had no choice but to accept her friend's decision. Kayla burst out in sobs and tears, sobbing as she hugged Hannah tight as if she would never see her again. Hannah assured her that it would all be okay.

"I will be right here whenever you need me", she cooed softly to her friend, "you are welcome to come see me anytime". Kayla nodded her head in agreement and her tears began to subside. Hannah informed her that she had signed the apartment over to her. The hugged each other tight before Hannah returned to her place among the other sisters. At last she felt at peace knowing that she was leaving that life that she was so unhappy with, behind her.

9 781801 341059